THE PAINTER'S WIFE

The Painter's Wife

ZOE MCGARRICK

Zoe McGarrick

Contents

For so many people I have known over the years this book
took for me to write, but namely:
Lydia, my best friend of the last 11 years, who supported me
through and through.
To Courtney, who had to read through all my typos and had
to figure out what an automaton is.
To Kyle, who helped me with any computer struggles (which
were many).
To Scott, who I wish knew his value and worth, and knows
how to brighten the lives of other when he himself is
submerged in the dark.
To my creative writing and English Literature teachers at
school, college and university, who helped my love for books
keep alight even in the darkest of times.
And mostly for the readers who love ghosts, gothic and all
things spooky who want to see this genre stay alive.

Content Warning

This book contains themes that some readers may find upsetting, and the author would like to warn you to proceed with caution if these are subject matters that have or will affect you.

The book does not contain graphic depictions but does contain implications and affects after and around subject matters such as; childhood sexual abuse, sex trafficking and domestic violence.

Chapter 1

11th November 1837

I had willingly walked through the gates of hell. The ice froze the ring to my finger, and my dress dragged behind me in the sludge, licking my heels.

Ice crawled up the windows as I peered out from behind the blood red curtains of the new bridal suite. New was a strange word to this house, though.

I was to remain in my wedding dress until he returned. The sun had long left me and the thought of him opening the door makes my skin crawl.

My husband has already left me behind the peeling walls of my impulsive decisions; a place where his mother eyes me like a hawk.

I've only been here for less than a day, arriving this morning after our wedding back on the outskirts of London. His eyes ogling me so much he became my something borrowed.

Just us. The vicar kept eyeing my white lace as he read the vows. When his eyes looked into mine, I glared at him, and he remembered.

The Baroness has harsh, striking features, a sharp nose and strong jaw. Her hair greying and pinned back in a vain attempt to preserve a youthful smoothness to her skin. Her clothes grip at her skin; caressing her skeletal frame into rigid movements that remind me of the clockwork automatons my mother forbade me to touch when she was alive.

Chills dance on my ribcage as I write about her. The Baroness. She reminds me a little of Mrs White, back at the Brothel with Meg.

But, from the moment I set foot on the grounds of Erlot Manor I felt like a swine being led innocently into a slaughterhouse. The naïve Pandora about to open chaos. I can feel something bad in the air, like poison slowly slipping into my bloodstream. The shadows are biding their time here. The air itself felt thicker, like smoke.

I was dragged up to the bridal suite after I had met my new mother-in-law, trepidation churning my stomach as I drew imminently closer to the finality of my fate. My dress strangling my skeleton. Despite the ice and snow caked on my boots, my skin burned under the lace and crinoline. My eyes darted around every crevice of my new home, my hair so tightly wound, like a viper, my temples pulsed. The sky bled into night; the orange dying into scarlet; greeting the darkness once more. All I can do now is wait. Just this morning I could have gone back to Meg instead.

His mansion consists of high grey crumbling walls – a stark contrast to the imposing home I had been promised when he had asked for my hand all those weeks ago. Now I feel a fool, not a bride but a court jester to his mother.

Dusk fell across the sky like a satin curtain, as we arrived at Erlot Manor, the cold winter air sliced into my cheeks, as my husband marched me towards the entrance, ready to parade me like a trophy. How ironic I should be stuck by myself right now.

While I wait for the land to grow darker, a crow caws in the distance, its raven wings a sooty smudge against the bare tree branches. The icy wind pierces its way through cracks in the wall, cooling my skin, drying away the tears that are firmly forcing their way through. What have I done?

The silence appeared as a familiar friend to me, the ache in my chest a strange comfort. I wanted to be alone after the journey, anyway. Stuck in a carriage, feigning delight for hours can make your face ache. Especially when your husband has as much charm and appeal to you as a slug.

Vomit churns and lurches in my stomach. I can't stop thinking of my own parents and their marriage. And what she had to endure. A faded memory, so what does it matter now? Misery remained a friend to her even in the fire.

Even though I knew I was his favourite, I still felt guilt stir my stomach that his wife never came first.

For all I know, my husband might be as careless as my father. He married a mask after all. Either way, my husband would return and claim me as his own, as he had done count-less times before, and then I would be a part of this place. I would have to live with my choice. As an orphan with no fortune, a prostitute no less too. I realise I am blessed to be a wealthy man's wife. That I should be grateful, as everyone in this family, or what's left of it, is thinking. They aren't the ones having him sweat all over them.

But now I am bound by law to the unearthly place of Erlot Manor. Its harsh wind, wintry tantrums and screaming storms are all mine to bear. Was this a better choice than that hell hole?

The room is a mournful delight. An ornate mirror smothers the entire wall opposite me. I can see myself right now, as I write, wide-eyed, pale, and ghostly. My dark hair is curled into a labyrinth. There is something stiff about me that I cannot brush off. As if the ring on my finger were anchoring my hands to Erlot. The metal cinching to the bone beneath.

The ebony wood of the bed is carved into polished vines that run and spiral along the posts, climaxing in a fountain of lilies and chrysanthemums at the crown. Red roses slump in a frosted glass vase next to the bed.

How romantic.

A doorway hooks my gaze. A moth-eaten tapestry conceals it, forced to grey. I warily turn the door handle. Until it clicks.

It creaks open.

The candlelight oozes inside and my eyes adjust to the dense darkness that stares back.

My husband's studio.

Portraits of his family engulf the walls of the mansion, each one judging me as I pass them by.

I brushed my fingertips over the rough edges of the canvases stacked at the back of the room. The details were almost life-like. Especially on the portraits.

My fingers are trembling as I grip each portrait. The ice in my heart cuts deep, chilling my spine with the poison I struggle to repress. The same lady. Dark hair, bright eyes, smooth skin. All ogling me intently; her gaze enticing.

My heart skipped a beat. I hesitated on a naked painting. Crude and real before my eyes.

The pile slams back against the wall with a thud.

I walked out.

Fresh air. I need air.

Outside the room, I felt like Persephone, dizzily tracing my steps through the darkness. The walls are nude outside this room. The evening shadows hang heavily in every room and corridor; obscuring my senses as I creep through the mansion.

She catches up to me. Just as I note my features are like hers. Dark hair, round pale faces, brown eyes. Except she appeared more beautiful and regal, knowing she was meant to be there.

The portrait is striking. Her beauty had been so cautiously crafted, so beautifully transferred to the canvas. The lady in question had a round, dewy face, rosy cheeks, red lips and mournful eyes that have been painted to hold an expression

I could not quite completely distinguish. The exact replica of the exposed lady in George's hidden collection.

The Baroness appears at the start of the corridor; the glow of her candles making the portrait more visible. The Baroness's face is so tight and concealed that it appears like a mask floating behind me. In this moment, I'm able to muse on how she has a similar composure to a crow; vigilant but patiently waiting for Pandora to slip.

"Who is this?" I inquire.

A moment of silence passes before she utters a syllable to me. I can feel her callous eyes burning a hole in my skull. "That was my daughter, Emily."

I study the portrait; searching her large, doleful eyes, painted to contain a mischievous glint. Her raven-black hair is pinned back loosely in a curled bun. Her dress choking her throat.

"Where is she? May I meet her?" I tear my eyes away from Emily's, and when I glanced back I could have sworn the portrait blinked.

"She's dead."

Chapter 2

MEG

Dear Meg,

After my years submerged by motherhood, Leo has grown to the noble age of four now, and, with the help of my dearest maid, we have decided we may be in fit state to receive a much needed and horribly overdue visit from you. These past few years have withered by like smoke and I long to see you again. This has to be the shortest letter I have ever written you, but I need to see you again. Please say I haven't left it too long?

Please write at once, I have made preparations for your stay immediately as I am fully aware of your requests to stay over the years, I only hope you feel the same.

The Manor has finally been restored to its former glory. I wish I may have torn parts of it down, let it burn and smoulder among the ashes where it belongs, but I couldn't. These walls hold pain but I hope that delight is not out of the question for future memories between us and also for my son. He is after all, my saviour, in the simplest of terms. Without him, I would have no Manor to keep you.

Yours always,
Rose Blackwood

28th August 1841

I wrote immediately, sending word that Rose would expect my arrival as soon as possible. I took to packing my bags the moment the letter slipped from my hands, sending it off that morning and praying no one would read it but her.

My bones ached with determination to leave this place, planning my subtle exit after my last client that night.

The buzz of girls giggling and rushing across hallways, beds bumping against walls, wet brushes slapping the floorboards to scrub the place clean was all alive in my ears again. I took a deep breath, trying to ignore the distant muffled cries of Adele next door, being comforted by Awkete. Adele had lost a child a few weeks before, but she had to work still, I suppose. Personally, I agree with Akwete, she should have more time to recover but the White's never listen.

The brothel was run by a married couple, breaching their sixties. A Mr and Mrs White. I never saw Mr White, except for a few instances as a child when they first procured me from the orphanage. Rose shortly followed and it stings bitterly to feel grateful that she came and guilty that I did not warn her to stay far away. Mrs White, however, was like a lipstick stain on a wine glass. She dressed in finery, you were kept in finery, the brothel was always presentable, but it could never escape what you were to them.

The children that screamed as they entered a cursed life. One that had you gasping in your sleep and pushed your backs to walls. You lived under her peacefully enough, you were happy enough. She was a cheerful, understanding woman but she never let you forget who you worked for, what you had to do and how much you needed her in return.

And so to ask to leave was impossible. She would probably laugh, joke around with you and then hold a shiv to your abdomen a second later.

So, no. I would have to sneak away. The only person I've seen White never stand up to like that was Akwete, who I'm convinced, after spying on conversations in my spare time, that Mrs White thinks she's some sort of witch, who would curse her with voodoo magic if she tried anything. I informed Akwete of this, but she only laughed and winked at me. I suppose she likes to keep it that way, their fear kept her alive and somewhat free. Just because her mother was a slave and her black skin told London every day, the Whites never asked her too much.

The London smog blanketed the streetlamps outside my window, a knock on the door, a rush of giggling girls and I swung it open to see Mrs White standing there, eyebrow arched, hand on her hip. A few wisps of hair had broken free around her forehead.

"Was that Lord Maxwell leaving?"

"Depends," I winced as I shifted onto one leg uneasily, "I can't recall him liking pain as much as this time. Perhaps he's switched names."

Her lips twitched, "do you need ice? I'll send Doll up in a minute. Get yourself cleaned up, you've a mornin' appointment tomorrow."

"Who?" I hobbled over to my dresser to grab a cigarette and lit it, pressing down hard with my lips to mask the pain. The bruise dug into my skin, seeping up from my thighs to my ribs. It had been a rough one tonight. My morning clients were a mixed bunch, though.

"He wants to be known as John."

I rolled my eyes, "how original."

She snorted, "how many John's is that for you now? It's gunna get confusing."

"You're telling me," I blew out a long spiral of smoke like a chimney, slumping down on my bed. "What's he into?"

"Wants a real lady by the sounds of it. Meek, polite but princess-y."

"He wants a doe."

"No, not a hunter, but probably wants to be a 'seducer' type, so if you could be ready by ten for that."

I nodded, taking a deep drag of smoke, burning my throat. I watched her leave, hoping to god she wouldn't miss me when I left. There was no way in hell I'd be letting some creep pin me down again. That was my last one tonight.

I waited till everyone was asleep before slipping out of the window.

Chapter 3

12th November 1837

My mind lingers on the doe-eyed portrait. Emily. She was so young in the painting, by the style I know it was George who'd preserved her memory behind thick oil paint. How could she die so young? The ghostliness of her pale skin made me shiver when I looked down at my own pale naked body. My eyes watching my chest heave, like an actress again.

Those thoughts vanished from my mind, when my husband lay on top of me last night.

He kissed my neck. His eyes traced the veins and bones my pale skin let him find. His wet lips exposed my skin like open wounds to cold air that slipped through the cracks in the walls.

Erlot Manor breathed with me.

The eyes that long watched this room gazed on the bridal sacrifice, but I lay there, shivering against the cold, eyes on the ceiling.

It was the inspection before the purchase. His last chance to throw away the poor orphan. Nothing he hadn't seen before. I was his whore for months previously.

I close my eyes, it will be easier if I imagine a happier time; when my mother sang me to sleep with a soft lullaby, or the time my father snuck into my room at night to give me a new doll he'd made me. I never liked to think of Meg in these moments. I felt guilt tug at my chest when I did.

None of those memories helped me relax.

The numbness I felt shift from my chest, spread gradually through me like arsenic.

I accepted my fate.

I am a Baroness, I am George Blackwood's wife.

I am his and his alone.

The only thought of rebellion I conjured was that he will never see me cry.

"Turn over."

I opened my eyes, brows furrowing. Again, really?

"I need you to turn around," he whispered again, something breaking in his voice. He was so quiet, it sounded like silk dragging along a polished floor to my ears, but an unpleasant iciness filled my stomach.

Why should I turn around? Isn't this how man and wife should be? I was still so naïve to think he'd prefer me the "proper" way.

George looked everywhere but me, only my skin, my hair, caressing my legs and hands like new sheets. From what I could glimpse, my husband did not want to see my face, he remained silently still, sat on the bed, next to me, both of us bare for the other to see. All he could see but my face.

All he wanted.

I held my breath, slowly turning onto my stomach and shifting until I was on all fours. I felt conscious of his presence behind me. The ghost of a man, that would soon claim me. I screwed my eyes shut, waiting. I pushed away the hands of ghosts from before. I wouldn't see them again, I wouldn't need the memories. I'd got the ring, the house, the security and yet I still had to do this.

I was clenching so hard, the pain soared through me and I yelped. He ignored but seemed to slow his pace at first. I held my breath, gasping when I felt I couldn't handle anymore. I felt numb, empty and cold. I was ice, my skin melting under his broken movements. Beads of sweat smothering my hips where his hands were. Iron clamps that bruised blue and purple paint splatters along my skin.

No matter how gentle the men could be with me, I hated it. The soft ones made my skin crawl, the rough ones left me bruises as payment. They were never nice. The most they could be was quick.

I shivered at his fingers dancing on my spine, but I never felt anything but the harsh reality that I'd set up for myself. The foolish orphan.

I was never an orphan to the Baron. I was only my body. Just like all the other men. Was that supposed to be comforting? I didn't know what was worse.

I remained still when I felt him leave me. I couldn't tell if I felt emptier. When a sob broke through the silence, I turned my head, sliding to sit down, I grabbed at the bed sheets, covering my modesty. Was he crying?

His back turned, knots of his spine screaming to pierce his translucent skin, his dark hair messy and damp, as he shook with a sob. Eyes wide, hands shaking. What did I do wrong? Did he regret his choice?

"George?" Nothing. "What's wrong?"

My voice floated from my lips in such a surreal way, I didn't recognise my own words. The room spun away from me.

I do not belong here.

George placed his arms in his lap, straightened his back and left the room without a word, tears clearly spilling over his cheeks. The door closed softly, his footsteps faded away, as my heartbeat softened.

Alone again. Alone and used. The air around me felt alien and cold. Only now did I notice the drops of sweat beaded on my arms. The roses beside me, his side, wilted more, disappointed at the lack of love they had witnessed; the lack of anything.

The mirror girl stared back at me, *who are you? Why did you choose this?*

Chapter 4

28th August 1841

I hoped no one would guess I was a prostitute. I do not know how they can, I wore the most clothes than I had in years. Like an actual lady. Like how Rose had ended up. I don't know if men can smell sex on you. I got some funny looks at the train station. Like wolves at night. Half the women I saw in the day had no idea who their husbands really were. They'd run for the hills if they knew. Or maybe they did know.

I stood on the platform far from them but kept my eye on them. Almost ten years of prostitution will teach you never to turn your back on a man, especially at night.

The train ride there was a dream. A wasted youth captured behind smeared red lipstick, ripped lingerie and burning liquor. And here I was, now bracing the countryside.

The trees flicked against the window, the moon racing me to Erlot Manor. I could never quite believe Rose whenever she wrote to me. Baroness of Erlot Manor. Baroness Rose Blackwood. How does an orphaned prostitute manage to marry a Baron? It must be true what Mrs White says, men go crazy for sex.

I had not seen Rose since she had begun her affair with George Blackwood before they married a few months later. He almost immediately kept her away from the brothel, renting her a small apartment on practically the other side of London. Far away from people like me.

Those dark brown eyes almost cried into my arms when she told me. I still can't say if they were from fear, grief or happiness. I lost her that day, she became a Baroness even then, and I remained some common prostitute to everyone else. I missed the way her hand would fit in mine and the whispers late at night, smothered by the sheets. I'd stare at her lips, wondering if there were clients as good as her. If I could stop thinking about her. But then she left and the bed was cold.

I lit up a cigarette, raising an eyebrow at a man giving me a curious look, as I blew a long sweep of smoke like a dragon, letting my stiff neck relax a little. His wife was in the carriage too.

Rose came from a somewhat wealthy family anyway, so she held herself high, chin never touching the floor, until it burned to dust when she was ten. We met at the orphanage. I can never help but wonder who had it worse. To know and love your family before they are taken away or to never know and only be thrown in corners or pushed onto beds.

One of the girls once sneered at me, telling me I might have been with my father here by mistake. I almost vomited at the thought. And I wish I had; all over her new dress. Mrs White made her client Damien Smith after that.

My stop came quicker than I expected. Darkness swept the land as I drifted off into the town of Eyreshire. It was late into the night when I asked a local carriage man to take me to Erlot Manor.

The deep lines in his forehead darkened. As if something were behind me, I looked around, already feeling the dreaded pit in my stomach unfurl at the thought.

"Sorry, sir, is it possible for you to take me there?" I chose my words carefully. Wary of the ways in which men tended to filter my words. I held a coin tightly in my hands, ready. I hoped he could. I dreaded the walk there to the hill. From the looks of it, a thick brush of trees guarded its entrance and circled it like a pit of fire.

From above, I was sure it looked like an eye, watching the world carefully.

Reluctantly, he accepted, helping me with my bags, and holding out a hand to help me into the carriage. I hopped in, and waited, the warm August air hovering against my face. My muffled hair ached with pins against my scalp. I felt somewhat like I was playing my newest character. Appealing to a different part of men; I was playing a lady. I sat back against a new canvas, the dark brush of trees ahead coating paint against a blank mind. Was Rose keeping herself away up here?

The carriage rolled along steadily, and I soon honed into the sound of my own breathing. Almost like low gasps, as I clasped my hands tightly in my lap, wary of the knife kept snug inside my sleeve. One eye kept on the driver and the other on the scenery that passed me by.

I hated the feeling that I was floating. Like if I didn't grip the carriage arm or the stone tightly enough, I could drift away. Like I wasn't in my own body, and these bones were pushing my soul away from them, disowning me. I closed my eyes and focused on each breath, fiddling with the knife handle through my sleeve like a rope to keep me anchored to the carriage.

The grey stone stood darkly against the midnight sky. Darker than black, some of the windows stared back out at the night, unwavering in its gaze. I let my mouth fall open when I saw its true expanse. The world that lay ahead of me. Rose the orphan, Rose the prostitute and now Rose the queen of a kingdom built from the ashes.

A light appeared in one of the windows and disappeared in the blink of an eye.

I leaned forward as the carriage stopped before the gates.

The gates themselves stood, curling in on themselves. Wizened by weather and curled into the state of a bitter hawthorn tree. They creaked at the slightest of breezes and greeted me with a gentle clang together, jangling the chain that tied them excitedly.

"Here," I stumbled from my daze as he prodded me with my suitcase. I turned on my heel and thanked him, handing him the money.

"Are you sure you'll be alright, Miss?"

I nodded and smiled, "of course."

He regarded me for a moment.

I arched my back, let my chin tilt up.

He left, his horse trotting away against cobbled stone that seemed to spring up somewhere near the house. As if you'd get lost in the woods and the path would be inviting you to Erlot Manor.

It didn't seem to lead away but to. I shook the gates, uneasy at the feeling Rose would forget I was coming. She must have gotten my message, I thought. Somehow, she must sense me outside these gates. My gut twisted and pulled my body closer to her.

Somewhere in that house of grey stone was *her*.

Erlot Manor was half new, half memory.

Crumbling stone wilted against new red brick. I shuddered as I let my gaze wonder along rose vines creeping up to windows unseen. Wooden panels criss-crossed against some of them. The moonlight aching to barge in. A light flickered at the window closest to the entrance, a curtain falling back before I could see who it was. The door unlocked and swung open as a small woman dressed in a maid's uniform and a man, hastily dressed, his white shirt creased and untucked at the back. She handed him her candle before he strolled towards me.

"Name?" He looked me up and down the way men tend to.

"Megan Marilow. I am expected."

He grunted, unlocking the chain and letting the gate swing open. I had to leap backward. I raised my eyebrow, picking up my suitcase before hitching up my skirt and striding toward the entrance.

The maid smiled at me and signalled for me to come inside.

"Are you hungry? I could prepare you a supper," she looked me up and down and a slight glassiness took her eyes. I shook my head.

"No, I am tired more than anything else. Is your mistress awake? I don't wish to disturb her otherwise."

"I am afraid Miss Blackwood sleeps at this hour," it was said almost smugly. "But your room has been prepared for you. I hope it is to your liking."

She watched the man behind me as she spoke, as he banged the gates together and made a racket putting the chain back on.

"Right this way, Miss Marilow."

I followed her down twists and turns of stairs until we arrived at a small room. The room itself felt a layer of dust, from being hastily aired out earlier. The bed covers waited for me and I stood hungrily aching for sleep. My leg still twitched at the memories buried in bruises on my skin of just hours before. I shuddered at the thought of hands crawling all over me like spiders, making webs and trapping me in them. The sticky webs staining my skin.

"Is it possible to bathe before bed?"

She nodded and walked toward a door across from the bed, I would not have noticed in this light. She disappeared, the sound of splashing water snapping me from my sense. I poked my head in to see her pouring jug after jug into a copper basin in the middle of the room. I smiled at her, "that's enough, I should be quite alright from here."

She left abruptly, too ready to leave for her own bed.

And I was alone.

I undressed, thinking how full my lungs felt when they breathed, how my shoulders could sag, and I sighed at the touch of the water lapping at my legs as I lowered myself into the tub. Lying back, a glass of scotch I'd been given as a night-cap in one hand, cigarette in the other. The bruises stared up at me through the water. I'd never felt so clean.

This could be my new life if I was as smart as Rose.

Chapter 5

ROSE

13th November 1837

I did not see my husband the next day. I sat on my bed like a doll, waiting for something to happen. The wind to change. The snow to melt. The crows to fly closer. Something.

Even the air was too still.

When I sat down, it stung. When I moved to stand, I ached. When I thought of my husband, I felt sick. Months without having to lie down with dogs, and I'd walked off with a wolf.

My surroundings sighed in boredom; the bedpost flowers wilted to match their cousins in the frosted vase. I, myself, remained a statue. What could I do? I keep writing in here to stay sane. The silence is deafening, it has its own noise, and I don't like it. At least at the Whites' there was always chatter. There was crying. But then there was Meg.

The house remained, in some places, unexplored. Without adventurous curiosity, I was pulled back into last night. The harsh numbness that came with the marriage bed and the tears that came from a husband. This was now my life and I needed to accept that part of it too, but the moment a part of it entered my mind, I felt my eyes narrow, my skin shiver and my insides freeze. Exploring the world I ruled, after the hawk-mother, became my only option. I have no other purpose. Especially to the Blackwood's.

The sunlight waltzed with the dust in the air with every window I passed.

When I was a child, I played with my toys near the window in the nursery. My father's creations clapping their hands, standing up and blinking. Each doll beautifully crafted. They would look at me with a glint in their eye. Once my father touched them, the light died.

All a blur to me now. I hardly remember their faces. When I close my eyes and try my best to picture them. Their faces are blurred away from me. Like coffee stains on an handkerchief.

Mother would hide each one from me when I slept.

Having come to a place I did not recognise, my heart raced. I was here. A place I could hide from the mother and my husband. It was somewhere far away from that room, now stained with the memories of the night before. My skin crawled at the lingering thought of his touch. The ghostliness of his presence even when he entered me, the pain was the only thing I felt. After that, I was simply hollow.

A tapestry hung limp over an arch way. Moth-eaten and devoured by time.

My interest spiked when I caught a glimpse of a staircase behind it. The red had died and faded into a dark brown, holes stabbed through. Dust burned my eyes with dust as I threw it back to reveal a large window bordered up with flaked wood and rusted nails.

The spiral staircase was before it. The metals bars curled towards me, luring me to the top where my heart dropped.

My mouth fell open.

It led me to where the air was thick and the snow had melted into the ice on the mountains. The light that could creep in led my gaze to a cradle.

The dust lingered here. A small room.

Grey and insignificant, hiding itself in the corner, away from me. Stepping into the room felt like I had disturbed a deep discussion between two people. The walls and the roof were watching me, judging where I placed my feet, how my fingers twitched, itching to understand why a cradle would be in the Manor, why it would be *here*.

Knitted blankets had the name 'Matthew,' stitched into them lovingly. Each curl of a letter made warm sadness well inside me. I had nothing from my childhood. And here was a childhood with nothing from it. When a tear fell and splashed on the red stitching, I gasped and fled the room, the eyes following me, until I reached my room. I slammed the door closed, steadying my breathing as I leaned against it.

This room, my room, was no better.

With the dark wood carved into depressed flowers, while the real flowers had been killed.

I wanted to scream at this place. Erlot Manor could never be my home. The coldness lingered, even in the sunlight. Erlot Manor was the only place where the sun became the moon through the windows. Erlot Manor was the only place where warmth became ice. Erlot Manor was the only place I could be.

Chapter 6

MEG

29th August 1841

I scrunched my nose in disgust as sunlight blinded my eye-lids red. The soft sheets curled toward me, as I stirred. The humid August heat tingled along my arms, sweat threatening to ruin the welcoming feeling of my bed. But I had to get up. I had no idea what time it was.

Once dressed, rouge blushing my lips and cheeks to liven up, posing to myself. Doing my best to ignore the butterflies in my stomach. I would see Rose again for the first time in over four years when I left this room.

When I entered the dining room, there she was.

I stood there stunned. Like lightning had come and struck all breath from my lungs.

Rose had changed so much.

Rose Mallory was gone and here sat Rose Blackwood, Baroness and mistress of Erlot Manor.

Her once shiny dark hair that hung down her shoulders in beautiful curls, her sparkling dark eyes, her milky-white skin and rosy cheeks were gone.

Her black hair was meticulously curled and pinned on her head. As if she had crowned herself. Her dark eyes were hollow and glassy when she looked up at me and smiled. Her milky-white skin had greyed and paled. No rosey cheeks to be seen.

Black lace had been strategically placed over her face. Sewn into the skin of her cheeks, stretching across her eye in an uncomfortable manner as it moved to caress her. The skin glimpsed me, singed and melted where the lace slipped. I pried my eyes away, now feeling the depth of her in the letters where she was torn from the loss of her beauty, at the injury she had endured in the fire.

"Good morning, Meg," she smiled. It did not meet her eyes. She took some time stepping out from the table and held her arms up. I held her tightly and briefly.

"I have missed you so," she whispered. The lace scratching my cheek.

"And I you," I smiled. It was still Rose behind the lace. "What has happened since I last saw you?"

"Many secrets," she winked, "nothing that could surprise you."

A glassiness returned to her eyes for a split second and, with her eyes trained on mine, I felt her stare past me. Black holes boring through mine. "But, what about you?" She glanced down at my dress and up again to my face, excitement, unpractised, scratching her throat. "You're a woman now!"

"I was before you left," I mumbled, a blush creeping up my neck as she kept watching me. A spark finally ingited in those pits.

I was still her first memory, her first kiss. That can never be taken away with any amount of wealth or husbands. But then a strain tugged my chest. She had left.

Those hands slid down my arm as we seemed to part from each other. A delicate, cold finger traced my hand. Porcelain on glass.

"Mama!"

She broke away in an instant the way a flame snuffs out.

"Darling!" She bent down and hugged her son, who bounded into the room and leapt into his mothers' arms. "Where's Belle? You need to stop running from her, you know."

"I wanted to see you, though."

He had her hair, I thought. And then I almost gasped. His eyes bored into mine like hers. Dark, round and full of wonder.

"Darling, this is my friend Meg, say hello," she stood up, turning him easily in her hands, that rested on his shoulders. He moulded against her touch like clay.

He looked up at me. His sun-kissed skin and rosy nose were a stark contrast against the dark and dusty halls of Erlot Manor. He was like a poppy amongst ashes.

"This is Leopold, my son," she smiled warmly down at him the way mothers often do. Her hands tightening slightly on his shoulders. A glassy expression returned to her eyes, her lips fighting to frown against the tide. "Leopold sounds like a gentleman, doesn't it? Like a hero?"

"Yes, he does," I smiled back, the little boy smiled back, drinking in the praise hungrily, the way young boys will do.

Chapter 7

ROSE

13th November 1837

There are people in this world that will hold you under water until you learn to hold your breath. I became the heiress to Erlot Manor out of a cluster of other orphan girls. He picked me but I made myself be seen. We have two sides to us, invisible and obscene. So, I taught myself to become an obscene delight. He may have asked me to marry him but I coaxed the concept into his mind. My own way out of there. My escape plan.

And now I am nothing but invisible again, obscene in the marriage bed, but still invisible. Worse... a ghost. I stare down at my hands, pale and luminous in the candlelight. Shadows dance against the frame, my hands still, but their darkness frantic on the polished floorboards. The world is hidden in our shadows.

A knock at the door came. Pausing a second to take a deep breath, I opened the door.

There stood a young woman, perhaps no younger than myself, wisps of her hair fallen around her face, pale blue eyes peering at me, as her hands twisted in front of her apron eyes darting around the room.

"Hello miss, I am to be assigned your new maid."

It came out like a question.

I raised an eyebrow; this was late for a personal lady's maid? Her pale skin sunk in at the cheeks and made her eyes appear bluer than they should be allowed. Her faded lips held a fast shade of red where her teeth had gnawed. I opened my door wider.

"Do come in."

"Thank you, Miss."

She walked in, eyes following the trails of the ebony bed frame. She glanced at the bed sheets then back at me. I remained silent.

"I should change them, Miss."

"Very well."

An uncanny sense of authority tried to creep into my chest, shifting around my corset until it held me tall. I felt sick but it clung on as she stripped my bed of its clothes.

"I will leave you to it, ..."

I waited for a name and she almost squeaked when she realised.

"Annabella, Miss."

"Annabella."

I left. I didn't know if I had to tell her or say goodbye, this new-found send of status fell on me like a brick. How do lady's address their servants? So this is the life I was meant to have before the fire? Flashes of bright white linens, fancy dresses, my mother playing with a necklace absentmindedly, smoke entered my mind, as easily as so many other memories, as if all of them freely walked around opening doors at will.

I'd read books with ladies in, but they never featured the maids too much. They were hidden behind the poetry of each page, waiting for permission to be in the narrative. And here I am, one of them, in the folds of my own book. A bleak story I am sure.

The grey day permitted Erlot Manor's walls to sag and sigh, candles had to be lit and carried down the hallways, before the house would swallow you up. Now that I was invisible, the house was hungry to keep me that way.

I fled, detaching a candle from the wall to accompany me. I walked with purpose, not letting the flame flicker on to portraits and catch my eye. The orange intruding on the wanton faces shrouded in black.

But then I stopped.

There was a portrait next to me of Emily. Only... she seemed young and vibrant. There was a sparkle in her eyes, a rosiness to her cheeks. I felt an uncomfortable lightness in my chest in catching her eye. My husband's paintings were so different to this. I couldn't stop my mind when it flashed with the naked woman. Her eyes were similar to the Emily's now, only there was an uncanny sense of sadness in the naked woman. I shook it from my head; it would be foolish to believe he had a completely celibate life before he married me. I very clearly had not.

Emily was only recognisable in her stare. Piercing, although much more intimidating, and her hair pulled back into a tight bun. How could it be possible to be stern, carry yourself with chilling authority, and have a vivacious and mischievous countenance? I had never seen a woman like this before. This was more confidence than I had ever encountered with femininity; Emily held herself the way a man does; aware of a mighty fortune at her feet and as if the world would obey her with one sharp look in its' direction. Eyes once so bright and full of life, cold and shrewd in the depths of Erlot Manor. Then it struck me.

How did Anabella get here through the snow? I found a window, and, balancing my candle on the windowsill, pushed the window open.

Brilliant cool air greeted me, desperate to float into the Manor and chill its skeletal mold. The ice held my face stiffly, but I drank it in, breathing in delicious cold air.

I have been in this prison only for three days, but how I yearn for the feel of grass brushing against my skins. To walk barefoot in the earth with Meg again.

Now that was heaven.

We learnt the meanings behind herbs from Akwete at the brothel, and go out in search, when we were allowed to, with the Whites watching us closely. I suppose there was witchcraft with us at the orphanage too, the way she would entrance me in her looks, too young to understand that feeling, but old enough to want to act on it.

How I loved to balance myself on the walls that guarded the orphanage. Me and Meg dancing along the pebbles by the lake, our noses bright pink and our lips devil red. Her hair framing her face as it fell from her tight hairstyle. Free from a world before marriage. She tied to her fate, I to mine. I hope she's safe. As safe as she can be, all things considered.

Before the orphanage there were vague memories of the outdoors in my life. My mother and father sitting stiffly near each other, my father urging me to play with one of his inventions, while my mother looked on.

In the distance the same crow watched me from before from the same tree. His stiff exterior rigid against the others, silhouettes against pure snowfall.

"What are you doing?"

I gasped and almost knocked the candle to the floor. But he caught it with one swoop of his arm. The gardener.

"I was just getting some fresh air."

He regarded me a moment. His light brown hair and warm brown eyes didn't suit the family of Erlot Manor. He was shorter than my husband, and slightly chubby, but the Winter months had not been kind to his skin and his hands were coarse, dirt biting his fingernails.

"Does George not let them out anymore?" He chuckled. I frowned.

"I can leave, but it would be a cold walk, don't you think?" I waved over to the snow. The house whistled in the quiet between us, as the gardener looked at me. I couldn't distinguish between surprise, curiosity and sympathy. I blushed thinking how the servants must know my fate' they might even have heard my husbands cries last night.

The wind slammed the window shut.

I jumped.

"Best to keep the wind out, Miss, house is cold enough as it is."

And with that, he walked past me.

Later that night I sat as Annabella brushed my hair. Her soft hands were gentle as she tried not to hurt me, it felt a sudden and welcome change to be treated with delicacy. As if I'd shatter if she touched me too much. It reminded me of the way Meg first kissed me...

"What do your friends call you?"

The poor creature jumped. She'd been so caught up in her work. A little smile daring to grace her red-bitten lips.

"Oh,... Belle." She smiled at me through the mirror. I smiled back, finally a woman I could talk to.

She stopped smiling and squeaked out a "Miss."

I shook my head at her.

"You can call me Rose, if you'd like?" I offered.

"Oh no," she shook her head, paling, "that wouldn't be proper, the Baroness said-"

"Are you under her command or mine?"

"Well," she bit her lip.

"I demand you call me Rose." I smiled, straightening up. I watched as a blush crept up her neck. A smile fought its way from under teeth.

"Okay... Rose."

She went back to brushing my hair and I bathed in the warmth that fought against the cracks in my room. The house sighed watching us.

"Belle, how long have you worked here?"

"Oh," she didn't look at me, "almost five years, but I've been here forever, I was born here."

"You were born here?" my eyebrows shot up.

"My mother used to be the housekeeper." She bit her lip again, now very obviously trying to avoid my gaze. "I was born in the laundry room one evening. All the maids helped look after me, there were a lot more of us back then," she laughed. "I've technically been working here since then, but officially as a Lady's maid for five, and then just in kitchens since."

"The Baroness?"

Belle hesitated. "No."

I looked down at my wedding ring. Cold against my hand.

"Emily?"

"Think we should get you to bed, Miss."

She didn't say anything else on the matter, I dismissed her from the room after she kindly warmed up the bed with a bed pan for me. Thanks to Belle's presence, the room filled with a more domestic touch, warming my stay. The black tendrils carved into my bed softened and the flowers lifted. I sighed, feeling, finally, at ease since my arrival. The moon peered at me from the window as I lay on my bed. Her footprints into my room beckoned me to look outside. I stared out at the pitch black. The full moon was the only light over Erlot Manor. No lamps dotted the grounds. Nothing but the cold darkness, the cawing of crows and the hard metal of a specific one in the trees watching me.

I recognised it then.

A shudder shook my chest and I almost stumbled backwards.

It had to be a trick of the moonlight. The hollow pit where its beady eyes should have sat never left its watchful gaze of my window.

It reminded me of the automatons my father used to create.

Chapter 8

MEG

29th August 1841

"I can see you in him," I said after a pause. The silence was smashed. The house edged away from the bright sun shining in the windows. The end of August marking the few last rays we would get.

Rose's lips quirked, but the glassiness in her eyes remained as she stared out the window onto the garden where Leopold was playing with the maid. Her back stood stiffly like a pole kept her upright. Her hair was frozen in coils on her head and the black lace disguised her expressions. I suspect that's the way she likes it to be.

"I worry there is too much of me in him."

I frowned, standing up from the dusty couch I'd been perched on. I took a tentative step towards her; she flinched a little at the change but kept her eyes trained on her son.

"He's lucky to have you as a mother," I started, unsure of the path.

Her mouth strained a small smile, looking over at me, eyes flickering over mine. She darted back to the window like a mouse.

"I suppose so," was all she said on the matter.

"This place is wonderful," I smiled, marching over to admire the room in full, hands sliding over polished wooden shelves, and looking into the eyes of portraits hanging tall above me. "It's like you have your very own castle."

There was that smile again.

"A castle waring away," she muttered, "soon I'll be as faded away as it."

"You're only twenty-five and already so dramatic," I rolled my eyes. "At least..." I eyed her, sliding a cigarette out from my purse on the table, "at least it's better to fade away quietly than to live in hell every day."

Her eyes sparkled at me; I could feel them on the back of my head. "Would you rather be a ghost then?"

"Any day," I said without hesitation, cigarette in mouth, lighting it quickly.

Another lull in the conversation.

"Meg, I have missed you so much."

I tilted my head but couldn't bear to look up at her. I let a sigh of smoke burst its way into the room. I prayed she couldn't see how my skin burned at her touch.

"I mean it, your letters have been everything to me. You write so honestly, so emotionally..." a pink tint spread across her cheeks, and she looked down. "I want you to know that, even if the years have changed us, I have never stopped thinking of you."

I glanced up. Her eyes burned with fire. The room faded away in comparison to the determination that shone through her. All the energy she kept locked tightly away was breaking through, like the cracks in the walls.

I did not reply, I simple turned and kissed her.

Her lips were soft and cold against mine. She did not move for a moment.

Breaking away, I glanced up at her eyes. She regarded me strangely. Her head turned to search the room before pressing her lips to mine. My hands found her waist, gliding up her arms to her face, she was like ice. Cupping her cheeks, I deepened the kiss. But then she pulled away. She stepped back to the middle of the room.

"We mustn't..." she shook her head. "Not in daylight, I-"

I nodded as she faltered, looking down, my face flushing crimson.

"I have duties as a Baroness and as a mother. If anything were to-"

"No, no, I understand."

I turned back to the room and took a drag, as if nothing had happened.

Chapter 9

ROSE

15th November 1837

Belle came and woke me the next day, I gasped when my eyes hit hers, gripping the sheets to cover me.

"Good morning, Miss, sorry to startle you! I didn't mean to," she tried to not look anywhere but my eyes, her cheeks flushed. "You seemed upset..." she turned to set out my clothes on the chair, "anyway, it's almost nine o'clock and breakfast will be over soon."

"I must have been having a nightmare," I mumbled, sliding out from under the sheets and trying to hurry with my clothes. I positioned myself at the bedpost ready for Belle to tighten my corset. We were quiet a moment, both aware that this was the morning I was supposed to seem more like a Baronness. The morning after my arrival I was allowed a day's rest (to my embarrassment) and then the next day, both my husband and his mother had left the grounds for town without notifying me. Today we would breakfast together as a family. And I was late.

"Do you often have nightmares, Miss?"

I kept my eyes on the crow outside.

"I suppose. I never really remember though. I told you to call me Rose."

I intruded the breakfast room only to be punished by the penetration of sharp dark eyes stabbing me the entire time I took to sit, bid good morning and take my breakfast.

"Do you often rise late, Mrs Blackwood?" The Baroness's voice choked sunlight that dared to filter in through the blinds. I felt a lump in my throat and looked down at my fork. My husband groaned at the opposite end of the table.

"I simply overslept, I'm very sorry for my late arrival... I found it difficult to sleep last night with the wind and the crows outside my window."

I watched her and my husband. George's eyes were red, blotchy and his face was pathetically pale. He looked the embodiment of sweat and I dreaded the next time he'd come to touch me. I glanced down at his hands and imagined them... like the others.

I felt a lurch in my stomach.

The Baroness, however, raised an eyebrow and there was something shining in the grey depths of those sullen eyes. That was all that was said in the hollow family room. The cold snow was no match for the people of Erlot Manor.

Before I left, my husband stood and asked to escort me across the garden. I accepted, taking his arm as he showed me the way outside. That was when it dawned on me, I hadn't known anything about the house for a full two days of being here. Erlot Manor had truly tricked me into being its prisoner. I wasn't Pandora opening chaos, I was to be a part of the trapped chaos.

With every step I felt my ribs strain against my corset. I thought tightening it might help.

I gulped air, trying to keep calm. The air cut my cheek like a knife, and my feet were lost to me. I shuddered when a blow of wind caught me and George to my hand in his clammy ones. I could freeze or be held by this man. Two horrifying fates.

"I understand you went to town yesterday," I almost accused him. He nodded.

"I had some business to attend to with my solicitor."

"And your mother had to go with you? Hold your hand?"

I tried my best to sound gentle. A jibe and nothing more.

I almost couldn't hold in how shocked I was at his appearance. The man was almost blue. Darkness stung the edges of his bloodshot eyes, and his lips were so pale they were scarcely visible. His nose had blushed bright red in the winter air. I couldn't help but feel this walk in the snow was an obligatory husband-act on his part. Was he aware my acceptance was of the same volition?

"It was a family matter."

I looked on, gritting my teeth. "Does that not mean me now?"

He didn't say anything on the matter.

"I must get back to my paintings," he smiled. "An artist never rests." He left me at the back of the house, wondering off to his studio, wherever that was. When I was quite sure there were no servants around, I sprinted to my room. Snow smashing to the floor from my wet boots, my fingers, toes, nose, lips and ears pierced by Winter herself as I rang for Belle to come up and light a fire for me. Prying off my boots, I flung them across the room, the thud bouncing off the walls. My toes melted as soon as they were free.

Five minutes later, my saviour arrived. Smiling sympathetically, she lit a fire, pried off my dress, where the hem was soaked. Placing a blanket around my arms, she guided me to sit in front of the fire.

"Thank you so much," I stammered.

"That's okay, Miss."

I smiled. She turned to leave and the thought of being alone on such a grey and dark day, shivering by myself clutched my chest.

"No," I blushed at how desperate and sudden I seemed. She turned, taken aback. "Please stay with me a while. Unless I'm keeping you?"

"Oh no, Miss, you're my sole charge."

I asked if she would read to me, so she sat next to me with a book and read aloud as best she could. Stumbling over words, she was butchering Dickens to be sure.

"Belle," she stopped reading, "I was wondering why the gardener is here if there is so much snow."

"Oh," she smiled. "I think he's stuck here for now. He lives a few towns over, but the snow makes the route almost impossible. He's had to stay until it clears up."

"I did wonder."

"I don't know what he's been doing though."

"Last I saw, he was skulking about the place."

She blinked.

"I bumped into him yesterday."

She smiled, her eyes shone, and her cheeks tinged pink. Curls framed her forehead where they wriggled free from her bun and relaxed. Starlight danced across her skin in the form of freckles. I felt myself lean forward and stopped myself.

"I suspect he's a bit bored when there isn't much to garden. But," she leaned in, whispering, almost looking about, mischief sparkled in her eyes dangerously, "he's been told off for being lazy and Mrs Blackwood has put him to clearing the snow." She giggled, "I watched him have to jump out the dining room window to clear the back garden path."

When I felt my bones ease into the warmth of the room, I stood up and Belle brought me another dress to wear. As I peered in the mirror, I seemed different. I didn't quite recognise my face. I peered closer.

"what's wrong, Miss?" Belle asked, as she cleared away my blanket and soaked dress.

I couldn't speak. I backed away from the mirror, a gasp lodged in my throat.

My dark eyes and dark hair, skin like snow but greying.

It was the woman from the painting. It was Emily.

And then suddenly my reflection was back and Emily had left.

"What is it?" It took me a moment to realise Belle was holding me and peering at me with those doe-like eyes.

"I... thought I saw someone else." I whispered. The wind howled into my room loudly and the fire choked. Staggering backwards to sit on my bed, I glanced at the mirror again, my own appearance pale, and ghostly like that of Emily. But it had definitely been her face I saw and not my own!

"Are you sure? Do you need me to fetch you some water? Maybe some brandy?" Belle knelt in front of me, as I shook my head. I could hardly speak from the shock.

The mirror watched me as I peered into it, I got up to scan the length of it. I was so sure I saw a different woman! But it could have been a trick of the light. Firelight casts many shadows and I was certain the shadows that lurked around Erlot Manor were ones not to be trusted. In fact, I was beginning to distrust the light if it flickered over my face enough to have me decide it wasn't my own face. No. I was here, and Emily was trapped in a painting. Two different paintings, in fact.

"Belle, you don't think I'm mad, do you?" I swallowed.

"No, Miss." She clutched at her hands, scratching the rash that clung onto her palm. "I think you're a bit shaken, though. Wouldn't you like to sit down?"

I shook my head, "I know you might think this strange, but can you tell me anything about Emily Blackwood. Anything at all?"

Belle didn't seem shocked by my request, but her rosy cheeks paled, and her teeth nibbled at her lip. "I shouldn't."

"Why shouldn't you?"

She remained quiet, her eyes falling to the floor.

"Has someone ordered you not to?"

When her eyes met mine, I had my answer.

"I won't tell anyone you told me anything. You can trust me." She didn't have a reason to, and, being a poor girl once, I knew it was a lethal decision to trust a woman above your station. The ones I'd met in my day were spoilt, untrustworthy gossips who married for silk and spread for satin. But, I can't say anything against them when I followed their lead.

"I used to be Emily's personal maid. She wasn't very nice to me... She died about two years ago now. I don't know what else you want to know. There isn't much to say except she died tragically young."

"Was she close with George?"

Her breath hitched. The circling chill in my room was slowly killing my fire and closing around my maids throat, daring her to utter another word to me.

I beckoned her to follow me with a wave of my hand, and, I showed her into my husband's secret storage room of paintings. She gnawed on her lip so hard she drew blood when I uncovered a naked painting of Emily Blackwood.

"Oh my-!" She gasped, hands flying to her mouth. "what... but- I mean...?"

"I found it on my first night here."

After a pause, "why would he paint his own sister naked?"

She looked ill. Her eyes were fused to the painting like a deer trapped by the light of a torch.

"When you asked me how close she was to your husband?" I nodded, breath held, "I think you already know the answer."

Chapter 10

MEG

30th August 1841

That night, I lay in bed, head spinning.

The moonlight stood coolly outside my window, as the humidity dressed me in lingering sweat. The sheets curled around my side as I kept shifting and turning, hoping sleep would overtake. But the feeling of lips on mine were like electricity and the aftershocks lingered like a ghost. I reached up to touch my mouth, my mind dizzy with the way she still tasted the same after all these years. The way my arms easily melted around her like candle-wax. How she kissed. Like she laced her rouge with venom, and it was driving me insane.

After all these years, she still haunted my dreams. I had hoped she would leave me, but those letters were like opium every week or month when I received one. To scrape desperately at my skin with my nails, scrubbing away the feeling of shame that men pressed upon me. Their eyes still left fingerprints and their kisses bruised mine. Hers were soft and delicate like she knew too much would kill me. But those letters lifted me from hell where I could ignore the flames licking at my neck and remember I was alive at least. That my heart could beat even when I was still.

Then a door creaked open and hushed voices interrupted my thoughts.

A giggle was stifled as a person walked away down the corridor. I slowly got out of bed, willing myself to float as I peered through the keyhole, holding my breath. Light staining my eyes as I saw the maid, Annabella, smile as she walked past my door. I frowned, wandering back to my bed.

The moon had died away from my window, and darkness swallowed the room. The bed creaked as I lowered myself down to sleep. I pried myself free of Rose and let sleep take me. If only it had been peaceful, I still feel in doubt as I write it all down now. Best I do now in case I forget something.

I shuddered awake.

The room was pitch black, the mirror on the dresses catching my eye as I saw my body, squirming and tangling in the sheets, reflected back at me. I placed a hand on my chest.

The bed creaked and I stopped. I wasn't moving. It creaked again.

There was a scratching sound underneath me. I looked to the mirror, but I couldn't see underneath. Only shadow.

I turned, edging to the end of my bed, my head hovering over the edge. Did I really want to stick my hand into the shadows? Instead, I watched the still darkness, my body locked above the dark. Could I catch a glimpse of it in the polished wooden floorboards? Would it creak below me? My lungs dared to move, while the rest of my body rigidly awaited something.

Just as I felt it may have been a trick of the mind, or just the branches scraping my window, it happened again.

A sudden scramble and a thud. Like it had flinched at my movement.

My heart was in my mouth as I stared down at the floor, body frozen in place against the pillows. Tears pricked my eyes, as I bit my lip to stop from gasping.

Then it was gone.

I waited, holding my breath, for anything more. Something. Anything.

But only dead silence greeted me, trying to weave its way into my ears.

I let go of the breath I was holding, falling back down against the pillows, looking up at the ceiling. Closing my eyes, I willed myself to stop being scared.

There's nothing there. It was probably just a mouse. Is what I kept telling myself. What I am still telling myself. But my words are weaker each time, echoing in my head.

I was dizzy, eyelids weighed down.

When I opened them again, a screamed died in my throat.

I turned fully to see it. Eyes trained, as if my eyes were keeping it in place.

A black figure, almost as translucent as the curtain was hid behind the curtains themselves.

A body.

Standing.

Waiting.

It did not move.

I did not hear any breathing. Nothing.

Just a body standing there as I lay on my bed. I felt electricity pulse through my ribs and tears prick my eyes. I dared not blink. I dared not provoke it.

Then the scratching sounded at my door and I flinched.

I looked at the door. Then back at the curtains.

It was gone.

I blinked. Only the soft dancing of the curtains was there. The moon poking its head through. Nothing else.

Whatever it was.

My heart pounded against my rib cage, wanting to leave as much as I.

I blinked away the tears. The silence had come again and sat up, jerkily watching around me.

It must have been a trick. The windowpane must had looked like a body. The moonlight shone through and all. It was just a trick. The scratching was a mouse. I need to stop being so dramatic.

After an hour or so of sitting there, shaking, eyes wearily resisting sleep, I drifted away.

Chapter 11

15th November 1837

I watched her. Her eyes were looking beyond me, dark and deep. She watched something with a smile on her face but there *was* a hint of sadness to it, I'm sure of it now. Her cheeks weren't as rosy as Belle's and her skin was paler than mine. Her hair was almost black, and the labyrinth it had been pulled back into was one to impress. It was a stark contrast to the seductive painting George had created in private. Her smooth pale skin would make the moon glower. Her eyes peered up at you through dark eyelashes, daring you to come closer? Or questioning why you were there? I felt naked when I saw that painting. Emily watched you in ways that made you feel she saw you.

She saw beneath your skin. Beneath your beauty. Beneath your actions. She saw your intentions, your purity and your sins melded together in a bitter wine.

I was being judged every time I saw that version of Emily. Instead of a labyrinth of hair, my husband had painted the black tendrils in cascades over her breasts, melting down her body in thick waves of charcoal. The beast trapped inside it nowhere to be seen. I preferred the less true painting; the one that hung on the walls of Erlot Manor and wasn't watching me. Like all the Blackwood's seemed to do.

But then my candle snuffed out. I knew I shouldn't leave windows open, the wind was fierce today, roaring like a lion against the cold stone of the manor. I shuffled around in my pockets until I finally found a match and, striking it, I caught the eyes of Emily Blackwood peering down at me.

I shrieked. The match dropped to the ground and the smoke travelled upwards like a snake towards her.

I looked up again, squinting in the dark.

She was back to normal. It was just like the mirror all over again.

"I see you're looking at paintings again, Mrs Blackwood?"

I squeaked, flinching, hand over my heart.

It was only the Baroness gliding towards me. Although, on second thought, the sight wasn't much of a relief.

"Yes, she... caught my eye." I calmed and peered back up at Emily. She had assumed her original gaze past me again. I smiled, but she just looked at me.

I shook my head and asked "how did she die?"

"In a tragic accident." Her tone was flat and I decided to not push her. The tight grey hairs that were pushed back out of her face shone silver in the candlelight like a knife.

"Could have guessed," I muttered, looking back at Emily.

Maybe she frowned at me then, but I dare to believe she'd let that much emotion through.

"I'm very sorry for your loss, it can't have been too long ago." With a small pause between us I pushed on, "I know what it's like to lose a loved one."

The thought floated out of my mouth and weasled into the ear of the Baroness, the taste of similarity between her and an orphan curling her lip like she'd just tasted a lemon.

"Perhaps it is time to be ready for dinner, *Mrs Blackwood*."

Chapter 12

MEG

30th August 1841

The next morning, I awoke to droplets of sweat running down my forehead, tears breaking free as I blinked them open, running to join the others at my hairline. I frowned, squeezing my eyes shut as the dazzle of sunlight blared through my open window. A cool breeze stroking my arms; I don't member opening the window.

I kicked my feet out and struggled to peel the sheets off, as I sat on the edge of the bed, my sheets clung to my body like a second skin. With a groan, I raked my fingers through my hair, sucking in a shaky breath.

When the night was gone, I could think clearly. Writing in here helps too. I decided it was all a dream, the silhouette, the scratching. I was used to vivid nightmares, after all.

I still think this now, but I should be honest and say I know it's more hope than knowing.

I drenched my body in a cool bath, the August heat taking no prisoners for another week.

I closed my eyes and let soft memories soothe my aching mind. A hangover of nightmares I called it. My body squirmed at the thought of those hands...

Stop.

I flinched, opening my eyes, staring behind me.

Breathe.

One. Two. Three.

My heart raced.

I am here.

I need to remember to tell myself that each time. I'm here at Erlot Manor with Rose. When my body felt like someone else's. I looked down at it, the water lapping over my legs and breasts, but I felt fuzzy. Watching myself like this. I moved the hand. It must be mine.

When I dressed and pinned my hair up, I found my way to the breakfast room, staring down at a cup of coffee. I took it black, watching idly as ribbons of steam glided towards my nose, the earthy smell warming my lungs.

I plucked out a cigarette too and had a deep inhale; two of my best companions.

"Did you sleep well?" Rose mumbled, as she sipped at her own cup. I pushed the fruit away, unable to eat anymore, the pit in my stomach was ebbing away slowly but reproachful to every mouthful.

"Yes, but it was a hot night."

"Oh, unbearable!" She smiled. That smile was the same. When Rose looked at me, I felt like we were fourteen again. When she slipped off the stone wall in the small garden, and I held her as she examined in the scrape on her knee. She was suddenly so close. Her hair smelt like fresh soap and her skin was tinged with lavender and cotton. I still remember the thrill that ran down my spine. I felt so connected to her, I didn't notice how she'd laced her fingers in mine because they should always be like that. Those dark brown eyes peering at me, questioning me. It was like we both knew what we felt but could not name it. I leaned in and pressed my lips to hers. It was only for a second. Little more than a peck, like a mother would give a child before they ran to school. But then she blushed and stared at me. That pit in my stomach was convulsing. She kissed me back.

My kiss was a question.

"Do you remember that night years ago, when Mr White had our window painted shut?-"

"And we almost couldn't stand each other it was so hot?" She giggled, "That was some heat."

Her gaze made me look down to my coffee again, trying to ignore that flush that crept up my neck.

"We had a few nights like that."

"Yes," I peered up at her again, heart swelling, "I remember."

The dark depth of those eyes lost me. I fell inside and felt darkness wash my skin, I felt searched, watched and the red balanced on my cheeks screamed for her to stop. When she finally looked away, I was sorry. My blood thrashed under her gaze, how would I be able to kiss her again or be touched? Being in front of her like this after so many years of hoping, of repressing so many desires, of picturing her on top of me instead of the men... My veins sang to inch my fingers closer to her hand on the table.

I'm so pathetic I just want to be near her.

Idle chat like a tightrope act between us, a silent promise between us never to mention the past. But my mind was dizzy with questions. I had plenty of time, unless the Whites were that desperate for me to return. They could find plenty women to fulfil my clients. A nasty taste flooded my tongue at the thought. I shook it from my mind.

Rose evidently forgot the past.

Her porcelain movements spoke years of practise and, as we sat delicately together. Her son finally being taken away to the garden. The breathing was so loud. As if it was talking for us. Puffing out from our lips: may I? Please?

I kissed her. I could have bruised her lips with the force. But she hungrily kissed back, biting my lower lip the way she did when she was angry. Would this be like that? Her cold fingers brushed the wisps of her from my face, trailing down my neck, like feathers tickling me. I gripped her waist, as if I were making sure she was really here, really kissing me. She pushed me back against the sofa, her body fighting against our clothes to press against mine. I gasp when her lips trailed down my neck, nibbling my collar bone.

But then my mind clouded over and as if waking up from a drunken night, I sat up.

"Why did you finally let me come visit you?"

Her flushed cheeks slowly faded, and her lips huffed out a breath of air, nostrils flaring.

"The house wasn't ready."

I nodded, "how long did it take?"

"Years."

I bit back another question. The air between us staled. Her eyes looked down at her hands, my skin burning where she had been.

"I would have come," I whispered. "I'd have come with you if you asked."

After a pause, she settled her head against my shoulder, her arms circling my waist. And then quietly, against my corset, "I know."

"I never-" I choked on my own words, stifled in my throat. Hot air puffed onto my chest, as we sat there, holding each other. Her vice-like grip telling a thousand stories she wouldn't let me hear.

"I know."

Chapter 13

ROSE

16th November 1837

That night I asked Belle to show me where Emily's room had been. One glimpse at its position near my own room sent a tremor through my body, I felt it circle my bones and settle in the pit of my stomach. A strange sickly feeling overtook me and I didn't need to be told how pale I looked. I already knew I was a ghost.

I stepped out of bed when I was sure the house was asleep. Slipping a shawl about my shoulders, flicking my hair out of my face and grabbing a candle.

The hallways were dark and still. Not a sound could be heard but my quiet breaths echoing back at me. I shivered and held my shawl closer to me. This house really is freezing.

The door stood prominently, the doorknob beautifully carved lilies circling the edged, almost sharp in the candle-light, flickering their edges at me like a threat.

When I touched the doorknob, I took a deep breath, heart in mouth, and turned to open it. It stayed shut. I tried again. It wouldn't budge. I twisted the doorknob until my knuckles bloomed white. I stood back with a gasp, shawl falling to the floor at my feet.

It was then a creak in the floorboards forced a gasp from my throat. Something had moved on the other side of the door.

I stilled.

I took my hand from the doorknob and stepped back, gnawing on my lip and begging my feet to keep quiet.

The creak again.

I bit down until copper engulfed my mouth.

Blinking back tears, I watched in horror.

The doorknob turned by itself.

The slow sliding of steel was like a twisting knife in my gut as I waited, rooted to the spot.

Silence.

Chest heaving, nails biting into my side, and lip red raw I waited. I dared to peel my eyes away from the doorknob. I felt the shadows watch with me. The portraits looking down on me. The whole of Erlot Manor waited for me.

Then, the door shook.

Bang. Bang. Bang.

The door frame shook. My eyes never left the doorknob.

It stopped.

With a deep breath, I raced back to my room. Not looking back.

Slamming the door shut, I held my back against it, chest heaving as I struggled to breathe. I stared wildly around, every nook and cranny checked before I could close my eyes.

Then I heard it again.

A creak. This time outside my door. I turned slowly around and faced my door. My heart leapt into my mouth as I heard another creak, further away. And then another. It, whatever it was, walked away.

I collapsed into bed.

It must have only been a few hours when I awoke to darkness looming before my eyes. The ache reached my muscles as I lay still.

I struck a match and lit a candle. My thoughts alive in chaos. The silence enveloped me, a lie in my ears.

A distant cry pierced through. I frowned, as I stared around, looking for some sign. There it was again. A shriek. Shrill and wailing far away and yet near.

A baby.

My heart flipped.

I got out of my bed and opened the window, peering outside, blinking against the dark that hung in front of my eyes like a mask. I felt my instincts kick in when I heard it louder and looked up to see a light on upstairs.

I felt along the walls with one hand, candle in the other, stumbling to find my way to the attic, each groove tasting my fingertips. Erlot Manor trying to work me out bit by bit.

I retraced my steps from the other day following a spiral staircase to the long-forgotten nursery. Moth eaten curtains greeted me. The crying stopped when I ripped them open.

Dust hung in the air. No baby in sight.

Only a crib. A dirty, wood-rotten crib. I crept towards it. The shadows scurrying out of the candle's view. Peering inside.

No baby.

A chill shot up my spine like a spider crawling along my skin and I held my breath.

On the other side of the room was a dresser something drew me forward. I ignored the mirror as best as I could, afraid of who I'd see. I pulled the top drawer open, fighting against the stiff mahogany, as I uncovered a blanket of dust. Picking up my candle, I let the glow catch glints of metal inside like a magpie. A key caught my eye and I pocketed it. Turning my back on the mirror.

My eyes bulged out of my head as I made no noise, held my breath, until I was safely out of reach of the cradle.

I hoisted up my nightgown and ran back to my room. I bashed my shoulder into the door with a hard smack, rattling the doorknob.

It wouldn't open.

I yanked and pulled, panic rising in my chest like bile. A pathetic wail choked in my throat as I rattled the door against its frame, looking about me, eyes burning with the threat of tears. Clutching the candle as I searched for the key before prodding it into the keyhole, but it wouldn't. I let a cry escape my lips before a cold claimed my insides.

Ringlets of hair plastered to my forehead, freezing in place, beads of sweat dripping from my head to my jaw, as I turned to Emily's room. There was a scraping noise. Like rats scuttling in the walls. I held the key out and slowly slid it inside the lock. With bated breath, I turned it, every scrape loud in my ears. It clicked.

The noise turned to silence the way a candle stops burning. I could feel whoever was on the other side.

I pushed open the door.

It creaked to a halt, the wide expanse of the dark room glaring back at me.

The windows pushed open to the sky. Cold, icy air hitting my face. The curtains billowed in the gentle wind. I stepped inside and felt the tone shift.

The curtains flailed, the window panes banged against the stone walls outside, and the moon ducked to watch me. The darkness held my hand to guide me inside.

After the chaos, what does Pandora do? No one ever wrote about that.

I stood in the silence, finding it twist the pit in my stomach and crawl along my skin a lot more than when there was scraping. I look down at the floorboards.

Scratches.

I bent down to look under the bed to find more. Words had been carved into the polished dark wooden floorboards. I bent down, looming the candle over the words, barely making out what they said at this odd angle. My back groaning, I pushed myself further under. My fingers traced over the letters. Blood had burst on some of the markings. Fingernails. Someone had scratched these words with their own nails.

MALLORY

I frowned. My maiden name. Who would do this?

I pushed myself back out of the bed.

A silhouette of a young women flashed by the window.

I gasped, blinking, almost dropping my candle.

She was gone.

Caught by the billow of the curtains.

Sick crawling up my throat, sweat dripping down my neck.

I needed to leave, I stared up at the bed, scared to see someone else.

No one.

I breathed.

I backed up and slammed into the dresser. I pulled a drawer open, staring at the room still, cautious of these shadows that followed. I dug my hand inside.

Who was trying to tell me something? Were they?

Or was this a message to leave and never comeback?

My bones ached for home. For Meg. But where would I go? I couldn't go back to the one place that took anyone.

I put the candle on the side and decided to turn my back on the room to find something. Anything. I frantically ransacked every drawer, tears threatening to stream down my face, chest heaving. I looked back again. Nothing. I was being silly, but I needed to go back.

Then something clicked. I looked back down at my hand. I'd pushed something inside the drawer and a hatch sprung open on the side.

I peered inside. A thick, yellow envelope slept inside. I let my fingers slip over and under, feeling the dust that clung to it. With the envelope in hand, I felt I'd come for what I needed. For what I hoped contained an answer.

With one last scan about the room, I backed out, slamming it shut and locking the door for good measure.

I lay back on my bed, my bones sinking into each other with a groan, muscle hugging limp limbs, and I closed my eyes. It seemed forever until I had the energy to move. My mind raced with a kaleidoscope of thoughts. One question after another but no answer chasing after it. I twitched my arm until it landed on the envelope. I slid until my back rested on the carved headboard, eyes staring at the envelope.

18th March, 1835

Dearest Emily,

While I'm away for a week, I can't help but write to you and pour my heart clumsily over the pages. I wait patiently to come back to you. I have almost finished your painting; I want you to have it and keep it. I made it for you, after all.

There are so many things that trouble me while I am away. I see so many men and women, hand in hand, here in London. They whisper to each other, the wife blushes and looks away. I want that and I want it with you, I don't care what the law says or what mother will say about it. You are my wife and that's final. God can strike us down if he disapproves so strongly of our love. My love is enough to conquer all your worries, darling. Are you ashamed of what we are? You could hardly look at me the last time we made love. You left before I woke. Am I just your brother now?

I will return to you soon. I want you to know that you are in my heart, my lungs and my bones. I think I should die if you were to leave me. So, don't.

Your ever-loving,

George

I frowned. There were letters dating back older than this one. This appeared to be the last letter he ever wrote to her.

His sister.

"So don't."

I shuddered.

MY chest ached in that room. Emily and I entwined unwillingly by Erlot.

She could hardly look at him when they made love like man and wife. And now he can't bear to look at me when we lie like husband and wife.

Every line is romantic and threatening. The pit in my stomach shrink away.

I chewed my nail as I rifled through more of his letters.

10th June 1832

Dear Emily,

I miss you so much. I am to be absent further, my darling. Do not let mother see this letter. Don't be as careless as you are with that maid of yours. She knows something and I know you talk through the night with her. What do you tell her?

The snow is getting worse again, they say when I do come home in a few weeks I may have to stay a few towns away until it clears properly. I cannot help but feel this is God sending me a warning. Am I safe to come home to you? Can I resist you again? I feel you around me always, your eyes are like firelight, they hypnotise me but I don't want to look away.

You have bewitched every part of me, and I do not know what to do.

I hope to come home to you but as what? Your brother or your lover? We can never marry, and I feel the guilt plague me every night I'm with you. I am sorry to tell you like this, but what we did was not a mistake but a sign.

But without you near me, I feel myself go insane. I don't know what to do, but I know I love you and I'm plagued by the inconvenience of it.

Otherwise, I am selling paintings. It's going well, you can at least tell mother that for me. There were some of you that have been highly praised, you'll be pleased to know. They see you as I see you.

Lovingly,

George.

Each letter either scribbled or determined. I could feel his mind whirl with right and wrongs. His slippery palms on this same letter. I felt him with me, but I didn't recognise him. This was not the man I had married.

He had fooled me too.

A double bluff.

Then a different letter entirely crawled into my grip.

The sun bloomed over the snow, shining into my room and glinting at the mirror. The rays kicked the crows off the trees and gracefully entered my room just as the candle I held snuffed out its last breath. I scanned yet more letters until I came across a completely different document.

A death certificate.

Emily Blackwood had died in this house two years ago from tuberculosis.

Chapter 14

MEG

1st September 1841

I raised my eyebrow as Annabella stood by Rose. Her face flushed every time Rose caught her eye or touched her hand gently. I felt a bite to my insides as I watched. She left the room, smirking at me as she passed. A breeze slapping across my face as she did.

"Is she always like that?"

Rose turned to see me in the doorway, before composing herself. If I had blinked, I'd be sure to miss it. Like a miniscule chip in a cup.

"Belle is so busy here, so many things for her to do in such a big house," she smiled, hand crawling across the back of the sofa. My mind flashed with a heated memory of us there, blood searing to push that memory aside.

"I was curious... why do you seem to have so few servants, and so many that leave after dinner?" the thought had only just entered my mind at that moment. As dishes were collected, and I settled by the fire with a book, flicking over the pages, casually glancing at Rose now and then like an agitated candle. I heard the door slam as the other two maids in the house left. I frowned and wondered, but the silence that curled around Rose was impenetrable and easily disturbed by questions. Any time I dared to ask a question, Rose's eyes narrowed ever so slightly, a twitch in her lip that signalled dangerous territory. It became clearer and clearer as the weeks passed them by that I only recognise an inkling of this Rose. Like ink in water, she was there but faded away and encroached upon by this strange façade.

Rose stilled her hand against the crushed velvet.

"Oh, they are such silly girls," she laughed, walking over to the window, where her face was hidden from view. The burning sun lit her dark hair up like fire curled and woven into her scalp. "they are children really for even being that scared, but they believe this place is haunted."

I let a chuckle breathed its way through my lips. I could not help it. Crushing pictures of the silhouette aside.

"I suppose that's bound to happen in an old house like this, though? Do the neighbours keep away and call you a witch?" I laughed, but Rose stayed close to the window, unmoveable.

"It is an old house."

"Why is it called Erlot Manor, anyway? Your husband's name's Blackwood, yes?"

I kept flicking through the book, not really reading at all.

Her back stiffened. "Yes, he was. His family owned this estate for a century or so, I believe, but the architect was named Erlot."

"Strange name," I breathed, letting my eyes drift away from Rose. Renewed energy from the firelight warming my skin, I moved about the room. My hands itching to play with all sorts of objects in the room. I could not help it. As a prostitute handling objects inside a clients' home helped relax me, it brought me back to the present, something to clench as they did what they wanted. I still carry around a small brass button in my pocket out of habit. Whenever a man was too rough for me to bare, I would grip hold of it. Crushing against my palm in my fist, sweat melting against it until it was over. Out of habit, I let my hand brush against my pocket to make sure it was still there. I suppose I wouldn't need that again any time soon.

"Yes, I believe he was French, but I have never heard of any name like that." Rose turned to watch me absentmindedly play with the small objects on the mantelpiece above the fireplace. A smile pressed on her lips.

"Anymore fun facts to deal out? Would love a history lesson," I smirked at her.

"I know he moved here and made this place after his wife was beheaded. That's it."

"Oh, is that all?"

She smiled.

"You'd make a very distracting teacher, I've got to say," I could not help it, I picked up my book again. She simply smiled again. "Anything else I should know?"

"I don't concern myself too heavily with the past."

I stopped then. I stared up at the wall, the clock was mounted and concentrated on the second hand. It flickered and did not quite reach its mark each time.

"Is that why you never answer my questions?"

There was that silence again. Ringing in my ears and I immediately wished I'd just bit my tongue and never said anything. I didn't want to look at her, but I also craved an answer.

"And what questions are these?" Rose sighed.

She'd opened the floodgates with those words. The room span. One look at Rose's glassy eyes, thin lips, and sagged shoulders told me to smile and be quiet.

"We don't have to concern ourselves with the past..." I bit my lip, regarding the way Rose struggled to come back to me. "You did mention, though, that you thought of me. Am I not your past, Rose?"

"You are," she breathed, her eyes slowly finding mine. A million words hung in the way not quite reaching tongues or ears.

I reached forward and stroked her arm delicately with my fingers, inching up to look her in the eyes. It felt wrong to try and kiss her again in that moment. I didn't know how else to comfort her though. Let her know she does not need to explain herself to me. Words were not enough for us today in that room. They never seemed to be for us.

As the evening took over, Rose left the drawing room to check on Leo. I felt crushed by the enormity of the room, the dust tickling my nose and the smell of burning wood thick in the air, heat smarting my eyes. The crackling of embers filled my ears and kept making me flinch.

Breathe.

I left the room before it became a different one. Melting away from the present and into the fireplace of another rich guest...

Breathe.

The dark hallways hung over me heavily, shadows curling against my cheeks. I shuddered. So many rooms I hadn't noticed before. The refurbishment was obvious on the outside of Erlot Manor. The bricks used fought with the grey stone for attention, enemies like oil and water.

On the inside, however, was another story. The cherry wood followed me everywhere. Polished floorboards bounced the candlelight back at me. There were no stitches like on a newly repaired toy. The past and the present were working together to preserve the finery of Erlot's architecture.

I found my way to Rose's bedroom. I hesitated. She would hate me, of course, but curiosity only killed cats. I took a deep breath and opened the door, sneaking in. I only wanted to glimpse what it was like. Was her room similar to mine? Truth be told part of me wanted to know if Belle had been in here or if she stayed here. I was only meaning to glance in and see. But it pulled me forward and there I was in the middle of the room and Erlot's walls watching me, knowing I'd broken some invisible rule.

The bed stood proudly, carved black wood, polished to perfection, against the right wall. Opposite was a wall-length, wide mirror that watched the bed. I felt a shiver run through me as I tried to stay out of its light. Then a doorway. I frowned.

Pushing against the wood, it swung open with a low creak. I bit back a gasp as a flood of dust itched my nose and I coughed and spluttered at the rude interruption. I should not be here. I should leave.

I walked inside to find canvases, facing the walls, stacked against one another. I eyed them warily, reaching out to pull one back and peer down. There was a naked woman.

Was that Rose?

"Excuse me," Rose slammed the canvas back against the pile and stood at my side, eyes blazing, cheeks a light, nostrils flaring. I flushed crimson, blood rushing past my ears.

"Sorry," I panicked, looking down at my candle, angrily thrashing in my palm.

"What were you thinking?" Venom sparked against her tongue, each word like a whip cracking. I felt the world wash away and her words lasso around me pulling me down.

"I'm so sorry," I felt the black daze pull at my eyes, blurring her. Where was I going?

My voice was monotone, and I tried to push more meaning back through my lips.

"I mean it, I should not have done this, I'm sorry! I came to find you, I-"

I felt tears rush to my eyes. I waited for her to yell at me, strike me, lock me away.

"Don't do it again."

I peered up at her, wide eyed.

"I won't."

She turned on her heel and held the door open for me. When I didn't move, she waved her hands impatiently. I felt sick. I wanted to leave. Tears pricked my eyes. I couldn't be here. I'd ruined another chance.

That night, I lay in bed thinking about the portrait. It could have been Rose. The same dark hair, pale complexion, dark eyes, but the curve of her belly was off, her legs were different, and her breasts were painted... it could have been the painter. Or have I forgotten what she looks like after so many years? My body shuddered at her expression. Wanting but a hint of alertness to the eyes. Poised. For what?

Chapter 15

ROSE

18th November 1837

Belle was helping me undress early the next night. I complained I was tired and needed an early rest, missing dinner with George and the Baroness. However, wolves trail after the weak and my husband was at my door.

"I heard you were too tired for dinner, my dear," he smiled, a weak tilting of his lips. Was this really the same man who wrote those letters? The same man who makes love to his sister by taking me. How the narcissus flower blooms in different shades.

I narrowed my eyes in search for the shy George who showed me his paintings when we first met. How his hair seemed darker now in the winter light, his skin paler and stretched over bone, made even whiter in contrast to his black suit and eyes boring into me. Disgust bit my lips and I recoiled my gaze, fingers twitching to scratch at the skin he'd touched.

I didn't want to be his Emily.

A dead man fucking a ghost.

I crawled away. Both me and Belle glanced at each other. Could I continue to undress with him there or did I have to wait?

"Yes, I don't know what's come over me. I feel awfully weak." I pretended to stumble into a chair, slowly lowering myself, with Belle to guide me. I felt his dark eyes on my exposed chest, my dress half off. Belle surrounded me with a shawl, and I engulfed my body with it, my head only visible to his wandering eyes.

"I am so sorry I could not be there at dinner tonight; I think it's this cold weather we've been having. Do you know if the snow will subside? I would dearly love to have some fresh air in town soon."

The Sun glowed red on his face.

"We are no longer snowed in, thanks to Matthew." He nodded, gripping his shirt sleeves.

Belle shied away from my husband's gaze, but I locked on.

"Is there anything I can be of use to, George?" I asked, letting his name slide of my tongue. He watched me slowly. I hadn't called him that except when I had been courting him. It used to light his face up bashfully. I could make his name sound wonderful, or I could make it sound disgusting. That seemed to be the only power I possessed so far as his wife.

"You've been so pale and ghostly these days, I worry we might need to call for the doctor."

I blink. Was that what he did for Emily?

"I don't think so. Rest and fresh air have always been the best medication when it comes to any ailment for me. And Belle," I glanced back at her smiling, "has been the best nurse I've ever had."

"Very well." He turns to leave. And I flinched.

"George," I called. Desperate or scared, I don't know how I felt let alone how I appeared.

"Yes?" He smiled, glancing over his shoulder at me, dark hair growing longer now that it curled out from under his neck like knives.

"Do apologise to your mother for me, I am awfully sorry about dinner."

I would ask again another time.

Once he was gone, Belle rushed to shut the door behind him, she even peaked through the keyhole, the light in the corridor shining a ray on her eye and cheek.

"What is it you're scared of about him?" I blurt out, as she moved over to me, sliding my shawl off my shoulders so we can resume getting changed. "You didn't look at him once."

"I've not met many monsters, Miss-"

"Call me Rose, for Christ's sakes. I'm not used to all this fanciness. I was born with you, not with them," I waved my hand, gesturing to the door.

"Very well, Rose." She loosened my corset as I stood, after I stepped out of my dress which puddled on the floor. "I've seen him be violent before. He's unpredictable."

I paused. Looking at her hands on my corset.

"What do you mean you've seen him be violent?"

"I was once getting the fire ready for Emily, he came in and slapped her." She blinks at the memory and I watch as she brushed the memory from her mind like a reflex. "He didn't say anything, just came in, struck her so hard she fell to the floor. Saw me and left." She took a shaky breath before looking me dead in the eyes with striking blue oceans wreaking havoc inside her, "I'll never forget the look in his eyes."

I turned away, "I can understand that."

I thought of all the times a man had struck me or the other women at the brothel.

After a pause, I asked, "do you remember why he was so angry with her?"

"No, but he probably didn't need one. Men like that might make up any excuse to be able to do that. I've read it in papers before."

I grabbed her wrist, forcing her to look me in the eyes, "I will never let him do that to me, don't worry."

There was a quiet understanding between us. The house felt it shield us, it's shadows not being able to penetrate the bubble I'd made in that moment. She regarded me for some time. Did she see Emily too?

"With all due respect, Ma'am... Emily didn't *let* him either."

Chapter 16

MEG

2nd September 1841

A cold sweat dripped from my forehead, crawling down my skin, pooling on my pale clammy hands, legs and pillow. I lifted my head, feeling a rush of air rest against my drenched scalp. I huffed out a breath, hand on my chest, my lungs were working double time.

When did this start? It took a while for me to realise the ache around my neck. I traced my veins tenderly with fingertips.

That was when I noticed the silhouette.

It was gone in the blink of an eye. But it was there. Am I here? Am I dreaming again? I threw back the covers, peeling them off my body. The cool air washing me, as I crawled up to the headrest, cradling my legs against my chest. I squeezed my eyes shut, tears slipping through the cracks.

Breathe.

Breathe.

Just keep breathing.

My breaths were shallow, short bursts. They filled my ears, merging with the rush of blood and the hammering of my heart. I clenched my hands together in a fist, as if I were holding a friend's hand. Clinging to myself for dear life.

When it subsided, I opened my eyes.

A hand lay above my sheets.

Grey. Faded. And sallow. The skin shined in the moonlight.

Fingernails caked in dirt and dried blood.

It looked almost liquid. A few more daring blinks later, it was there. Solid. On my bed.

As if someone were under my bed, and their hand had crawled on top, steadying themselves to push themselves up any minute now.

My heart pulsed in my ears. My body shuddered. A hollow breath burned into my lungs.

A sob caught in my throat and I bit my lip to stop myself. As if being silent would make it go away. Moving would agitate it. Making any sort of noise would make it crawl toward me.

Akwete used to say spirits left you alone if you left them alone.

I wanted to call out to someone, anyone, but who would come? Would the hand reveal an arm, then a shoulder, then a neck, then a face?

I waited, watching, a deep breath churning in my lungs, almost prying free of my ribcage as I waited. The silence hung between us, and tears rolled down my cheeks.

The hand twitched.

A whimper escaped my lips and I smacked a hand over my mouth in horror. I watched with wide eyes like a deer trapped in the headlights.

The hand's fingers slowly scrunched up toward the palms, fingers tips clenching around my discarded bed sheets, pulling them further away from me. A scream stirred in my chest.

Then there was that scraping sound again. Fingernails against wooden floorboards, I realised, trying to keep the tears in my eyes from blurring my vision.

Another hand crawled its way up the bed, lying beside the other one. Both stopping any movement. Dormant.

Breathe.

The bed creaked with the weight.

They inched forward like white tarantulas.

I could not move.

I was pinned against the headboard, the cool mahogany like fire against my skin.

Then they shook, squeezing the bed sheets.

I felt my blood churn, as they threatened to grip me like that. Bile rose in my throat.

Then a giggle sounded in the corridor and I flinched, jumping further up the bed. I turned my head quickly to the door, where candlelight flickered, lighting up the doorframe. Then back to the hands.

Gone.

All that was left, all the proof I had to remain focussed on, was the clenched circles left by the fists in my sheets.

Chapter 17

ROSE

19th November 1837

I tied the bright red ribbon under my chin tightly. My tight black curls that hung loosely about my forehead strove to make it look redder, and the hazel in my eyes shone through, I felt pretty looking at myself but was that because I looked distinctly less Emily in that moment? I looked juvenile and couldn't help stopping myself smiling, always striving to look older, more mature.

I left Erlot Manor with Belle that day for town, the carriage sliding along the snow until we came to a halt.

The town of Eyreshire was cleared of any and all snow, much to the dismay of the schoolboys who had seemingly run into the middle for a snowball fight, only to then wander off to the forest and woods to play. I watched all around me. It is a strange feeling to contain within yourself, when you have been cooped up inside with only one person to truly talk to and then be brought out into the middle of society as a lady. Some people looked at me oddly as I walked past, Belle frowned at them.

"Why are they looking at me like that?" I asked when we stopped for tea.

"I don't know," she shrugged. We hoped Belle looked the part of a lady enough to fit in at the tea rooms, but some of the people recognised her. When I made it clear she was my personal lady's maid they seemed satisfied enough. I watched her for a minute. Some people still seemed funny about it, but I felt too new to know why.

"Do I look like her?"

"Like who?" She said, watching the people walk past outside.

"Like Emily Blackwood." I raised an eyebrow.

She sighed, slowly and reluctantly tearing her eyes away from the pedestrians. "Yes."

I hadn't fully believed it to be true. It is an entirely new shock when someone confirms your worst fears. It wasn't me who placed myself into the church that day with George. It wasn't me who married him but fate. She'd watched and courted me, pulled me to him and dressed him as my opportunity. But was my fate a clone of Emily's? Was I to die so young and with child? Was I to have my painting locked out of sight?

"I know she had an affair with my husband, I know she had a baby with him, and I also know she died in that house." Her eyes peaked all around her, begging me to be quiet. "She died so young..."

"You don't understand. Society here doesn't know." She whispered quickly, warming her red raw fingers on her teacup. "Emily Blackwood never had a child as far as anyone outside of Erlot Manor is concerned. I'm just her maid, I couldn't do anything so don't look at me like that."

"How did she hide having a child with him from everyone?"

I wondered if Belle was ever going to speak. She seemed to have sewn her lips shut, eyes working away behind closed lids. Finally, they snapped open, and she whispered, "she didn't."

"Is that when *she* found out?" Meaning the Baroness of course.

Belle frowned, "I think so, but how it is possible to not know, with no other people in the house, really, to not notice *anything* strange between your own children?" She shook her head.

"You noticed."

"I was with Emily every waking moment," she smiled softly, glancing at me, "you know how lonely it is in that place."

I glanced down at my tea, knowing too well that the cold depths of the house of Erlot Manor were still a dream to whatever destiny would have done to me at the brothel. My mind bit harshly in remembrance of Meg, her cries in the night like a wolf-pup howling for its mother. Only no one came but me. Soft eyes forced wide with bloodshot and red raw. She whimpered in my arms that night they told her what happened. What would be happening to her again and again. The orphanage was a fiery pit even Tartarus would flinch from. Erlot Manor was simply a snake pit.

The next day they took her from me again and she stayed away until I later joined. If I was to go to Hell I would do it holding her hand.

With the watchful eyes and gossiping whispers around me, I couldn't help but yearn for Erlot. A strange sense of belonging had attached me to it; out of obligation, resolve or respect, who knew?

I placed the teacup to my lips and took a long sip, swirling the drink around my mouth while I thought. I missed the taste of whiskey burning my throat. Or wine those late nights giggling with Meg, hidden under the window, as we took turns spying on passers-by.

The Baroness must have known. She never struck me as a stupid woman. She was smarter than George.

"She was six years older than him, by the way."

"What? But she looks so young in her portraits!" My mouth hung open.

"Portraits are never honest," she sipped her tea. "And painters are too romantic for the truth."

I bit back a smile, looking into those bright blue eyes. There was a sparkle back there, it had been snuffed out time and time again but there was oxygen breathing it out now. "You're quite wise beyond your years, Belle."

She grinned like a wolf. "I used to stay up every night reading anything Emily had loaned me from her private library. She used to tell me it was always important for a woman to keep her mind sharp. I don't know if that's entirely true anymore..."

"I think, in light of the circumstances, that is all I or you can do right now..." I scrunched my nose, "we have to be his wife and maid. There's nothing to say or do except be ignorant."

She frowned, "what they did was horrific, and you don't really believe Emily simply died."

"We have no proof and it's not like they're committing incest *now*."

Belle glanced down, and I bit my lip, leaning forward to take her hand, "I'm sorry, I didn't mean it like that." After a moment, "there's something wrong in Erlot Manor, I know there is, I keep..."

I kept thinking do I tell her? Would she think I'm crazy? I wasn't entirely sure if I was daydreaming, placed in a new dark corner, figuring out where I actually am. The strange noises, these strange ghosts could all be in my head. An excited and aroused imagination. A conscience desperate for a reason to leave my own Fate.

"Please understand, he won't want you for too long."

I flashed my eyes to hers, so serious was her tone, the light-heartedness ripped from her like a daisy in a field, plucked to be kept and enjoyed by someone else. I swallowed, understanding itching in my veins like it did not belong, like I was rejecting the very notion being fed to me like poison.

I may look like Emily, but I was not her. And soon another girl would hold a closer resemblance.

Chapter 18

MEG

3rd September 1841

"You're not usually so quiet?" Rose appeared by my side, snapping my mind from whatever blurry pit it was falling into. I looked up from my hands. She had that childish sparkle in her eyes again. It was no wonder she had been lucky enough to escape the White's.

Her dark curly hair framed her slender pale face, her dark eyes were sultry. And she looked at you like she knew your secrets before meeting you. Her soft lips were pale, but she was to pick up on rouge when she needed richer clients. She was paler now. Living in solitude, I supposed you didn't need to wear a mask. Her husband was gone after all.

"Sorry, I'm quite tired, I didn't sleep well last night."

"I'm sorry to hear that," she brushed my blonde hair out of my face and behind my ear. Her fingertips lingered on my neck a second longer than they should have, and my heart leapt at the suspense. "Do you still have nightmares?"

I glanced at her mask; the lace just close to scraping her eyelid. Did she mind me looking?

It was little more than a whisper. A secret between us. We shared the same dreams this way, as we'd shared the same fate. Or had until she cut her ties and climbed the social ladder. I could never bite down the fears the way she could.

"Yes," I breathed, looking away. She slid her arms around my waist and pulled my into a side-hug. Her lips pressed against my cheek softly. Like a ghost.

"Do you want to know how I cope with them?"

I nodded, my throat closing. She laced her fingers in mine and I gripped back for dear life. Vertigo stained my vision slowly like a mist.

"I push my nail into my side like this." She demonstrated, breaking her hand from mine to press into her hip. "That's how I know I'm not there anymore. I can do that to myself... they can't anymore."

I breathed slowly, as we caught each other's eyes.

Her lips parted, brow furrowing, skin paling, like she was fading from view.

"Try it, darling," she cooed, leaning in until we were inches apart. My eyes flicked down to my hands, shaking in my lap. My hand lifted, rising to my hip and pinching, which, over the material of my dress, took some force to feel. When I did, it was like my vision cleared slowly. A disturbance in the blur, like I'd shocked my eyes into the presents. Lightning striking the mind.

I was here. Next to Rose. I closed my eyes, feeling less and less dizzy as I inhaled. She smelled like lavender and roses. Like melted butter from breakfast and a hint of coffee that still lingered on her breath. I smiled, turning to face her.

"Feeling better?" she asked, her face still serious and sombre. She was still my Rose.

I kissed her. Only softly and quickly. But a quick peck to her lips sent a jolt through my ribcage.

"Thank goodness," she smiled. Eyes shining back into mine like a sweet sunset.

After a pause, I looked away. The hands flaring up in my mind.

Cold, limp, dead.

That was real. That had happened.

"Rose, I know you think those maids are silly but..." I bit my lip, face heating up, "do you believe in any sort of afterlife?"

"Like ghosts?" She stiffened in my hands.

"Yes, do you think they exist, or something lingers after we go?"

I watched her eyes become a kaleidoscope of unreadable emotion. A flicker of worry, skepticism, concern, anxiety and then a dullness emptied the rest. "I can't say it is healthy to indulge in the idea."

"Is that a no, then?"

She said nothing. Only sighed, lifting her body away from mine, face turning to stare out the window. The white sunlight lit up her dewy skin like the moon itself. I felt my heart flutter when she turned to see me again. I decided to ask something else.

"You said I could ask questions the other day..."

"On the account I don't have to answer."

"Of course," I eyed her warily. "Why... do you never mention your husband?"

She stiffened, turning back to the outside world. A distance place to me now. There was the world and then there was Erlot Manor. An eerie comfort of old times. There were the men with the rough calloused hands, never stopping to look into your eyes unless it was to laugh, and then there was the soft but desperate embrace of Rose's arms. The shadows could curl up beside me all they liked, but I kept them at bay with the feeling of Rose.

"It seems so strange to me, you became a Baroness over-night-"

"He wanted me." She bit.

There was a pause.

"You know as well as I do, or thought, it is best to marry well and leave behind the past," she turned to face me, arms crossed against her chest, "so I did. But now he is dead and that, again, has become a past I need to forget."

"You still live here."

"Yes, but-" she bit her lip. I held my tongue. It seemed strange to stay in the home of your pain, whatever had happened, but I supposed I stayed that way too. Did the past have to matter?

I felt the cracks in the stone walls sing as the wind lashed across the windows, rain whipping the rocks and panes. Grey clouds blackened above the trees, their leaves rustling, whispering amongst each other. I watched. Leo ran inside.

"He'll catch his death doing that," I muttered, nodding toward the garden. Rose turned and saw her son.

In a second, she was out the door.

I lingered by the side of the window, hidden by the curtain, Belle beckoned for Leo to come in, obviously agitated; back stiff, finger pointing to her side. He giggled and ran from her the way children often do. Everything a game.

Belle held her hand out, standing still. I could not see her face. I could not hear her voice.

But Leo stopped, staring at her face. Slowly he walked forward, stumbling like a baby dear, and placed his hand in hers. They turned and I saw the wet sombre face of the maid. She looked down on him devotedly. I realise now, writing this and thinking about how soft her eyes really do become when she sees him, how much she loves and dotes on him.

I followed the twisting hall to linger near the entrance, cold stone against my hands and chest.

"Leo, we come inside immediately when it rains, you could get sick!" Rose was scolding the poor boy. And like a mother, she folded immediately after seeing his childish glee fall into sudden sadness that resembled her own glassy eyes. "I'm sorry, darling, it's okay, mummy's not really angry at you."

She looked up Belle, "run him a bath and make him up a fire in the nursery, we will be up shortly."

Rose turned to her son, "what were you doing?"

"I was playing! I made this!" He held up a man constructed of sticks, cloth and string.

Rose was quiet a moment, hands gingerly cradling the toy. She paled. "What have I said about this?"

"It wasn't painting, I swear!"

"Leo, listen to me. You know how I feel about … this," she practically spat the words. "You can write if you want to, why don't I get you some paper?"

"I just made him from sticks, it wasn't art or anything," his face fell, and he pouted at his stick man.

"Leo, remember what I said about this sort of thing. You don't want to be a dishonest person, do you?" Her words churned my stomach. So strange and sweet was her voice.

The child glanced at his shoes, which were shiny with rainwater. He shivered.

"Don't be an artist, Leo. Don't go near them." She crouched down in front of him, holding his shoulders, trying in earnest to force his eyes upon hers, her voice like a breath in his ear. "They can't help projecting their darkness onto people, stay away from temptations such as these, my darling."

I frowned. Rose sounded so desperate. In the weeks I had been staying at Erlot Manor, Rose had never sounded so frightened as she did now. I watched as Leo nodded solemnly, and Rose locked her arms around him like a cage.

"Oh no, I'm all wet too now!" She smiled, and Leo smiled. His childish joy did not bounce back, though.

Chapter 19

ROSE

1st December 1837

That was when I started being drugged.

The Baroness, I began feeling as if she had no other name, came to me, and started asking if I was unwell. I struggled to sleep most nights, sweating out the infestation of shadows that slid into my mouth, eyes and ears. Whilst fighting for my life, I'd be lying in wait for my husband to take me again. It had been a week since he'd defiled me. And sure enough, he was at my door.

I glanced at the bottle of pills. The sedatives. They'd help me sleep. I took one and lay down for him. I blew out the candle. It would disguise any part of myself from him. In the darkness I could become anyone he wanted; the arrangement sorted us well.

He'd dream me up to be Emily. With my help.

That was when the sedative left me limp and dazed, his harsh puffs of air in my ear moistened my skin and I turned away, watching the window, and then the mirror.

My own lost eyes gazing into mine. Then it was her. Emily watched through me. I could become her in the darkness. She crawled into my skin like a bed, and I leaned over his shoulder to watch her, the room wobbling away from me with the power of sleep sinking me lower into the pillows, further and further away from him and the marriage and Erlot. My hands on his arms. They seemed different. Paler.

I whispered into my husband's ear, "am I her?"

He flinched, jumping back from me. He regarded me with pin-prick eyes. I watched him, sleep blurring him from me, I was taken to a different place to him and thankful for it. His heart was pounding, deafening in my ears. Or was that my own heart? Or could it be Emily now? Did she really take my body or was she trapped in the mirror the same way she's trapped in his paintings? The same way I'm trapped under him, his slimy skin sticking to mine.

I awoke to Belle covering me with the sheet, her face bright red, "where'd he go?" I yawned.

The sheets were curled, damp and ultimately, I shoved them off me, sitting up and holding my face in my hands. The past six years in a brothel surrounded by other nude women, I didn't much care if Belle saw me. But I felt nausea stir at the eyes on me. And I was sticky.

"I need to bathe."

"Yes, of course."

Belle ran me a bath, splashing the tub with every hot jug of water, towels were brought in by other maids and I asked them to leave me.

"Except you, Belle," I smiled as best I could. I felt my skeleton sag and my mouth strain to smile. She held my hand as I stumbled into the bath, her eyes up at the ceiling. I was bolder now, but this was not my body. It wasn't Emily's either.

I splashed water into my face. Again. And again. The room was still not quite still nor was I moving as fast as normal. I sighed.

"Those sedatives are strong." I laughed. "Perhaps they've taken to poison-"

Belle threw them out of the window.

"Hey!"

"They *are* trying to poison you!" She breathed, container still in her grip, as she turned to me fiercely.

I slipped and slid in the water until I faced her, the tub squeaking and water half on the floor. The cool air from the open window striking my wet skin with a vengeance.

Curls escaped from her bun, and she shook her head, tears coming to her eyes.

"I was so blind before," she whispered. Her voice choked and she crumpled to the floor like paper.

Hands shaking, I steadied myself on the edge of the tub, sliding one leg at a time onto the smooth, polished floorboards. My feet grew hot with the anticipation that I was certain to fall over, my hands fizzed as sweat threatened its way to the surface. I grabbed for my silk robe and crawled to her. My breathing getting more and more laboured. My insides were curling together like a weight.

"It's okay," I cooed, sounding more forceful than I wanted. "It's okay." She did not move. I slid my hand into hers, bath water leaking in the cracks of our fingers.

I pried the container from her hands and slammed my thigh next to her, trying to sit comfortably. I watched her, sliding the hair that clung to my skin out of my face. "If there's one thing you are not, it's blind. I think," feeling just how weak I actually was since leaving my bed this morning, "I think you've saved my life, Belle."

She glanced up. Teary-eyed, bashful. "I didn't save *her*."

So, it wasn't tuberculosis.

There was a quiet I could feel in my dazed head.

"Come on, I have a task for you. We can do good by Emily, if you help me."

She didn't move, blinking so hard her forehead scrunched up, looking away from me. The tears streaked down her cheeks as if in a race to not be seen. I caught one and wiped it away.

Meg never cried quietly. Not that night. She probably does now.

I glanced at my door, "Emily, I need you to help me avenge Emily, your friend." I kept my voice lower than a whisper, finally understanding Belle. All the nervous glances my way, all the submission to the family, the watching through the keyhole. Belle knew the poison in Erlot Manor better than anyone. She was the only one doing her best not to breathe it in.

I was about to repeat myself when her brow softened, and her arms unfolded, like she was a delicate moth born from its cocoon. I called for some tea and helped her by the fire.

When the tea arrived, I balanced it on the table before her and wrapped her in a blanket, her eyes still staring down at her lily-white hands, soft and pale as petals in my own.

"It's okay, Belle, really. Please," I held a cup and saucer of tea under her nose, "have something to drink, you'll feel better."

She took the cup with shaky hands, and, after a sip, seemed to pour life back into her gaunt and stunned doe-eyes, roses blooming on her pale cheeks once more. I smiled, sitting back on my heels.

"I didn't know how you took it-"

"Oh, I shouldn't be the one drinking your tea!" She squeaked, jumping up, the blanket falling down behind her. "I was giving you a bath!"

"No, don't worry about that yet!" I laughed, "saving my life is a far more honourable task after all!"

Her face grew crimson, the blues in her eyes popping out of her skull. She glanced down at the tea and bit her lip.

"Look, think of me as just another woman with you, not your mistress." I watched her face slowly trace up my body to meet my own. "Have tea with me as a friend for a moment, or I'll order you as my maid to."

She smiled weakly and sat back down, hastily sipping. Her lips drew down and she blinked a moment too long.

I winced, "I did say I didn't know how you take it! I'm not a big sugar person."

"No milk either, apparently," she giggled. "It's okay," she soothed me, her sweet smile returning to her lips as she leaned over to plop three sugar cubes and milk to her tea.

After a moment of awkward silence had passed between us, the flames in the fire crackling happily at us, I bit my lip and asked, "I thought you said Emily was... not a nice employer?"

"Hmm," she hummed against the lip of her cup, placing it slowly back down with a clink. "Well... please don't find me making too general a statement, but... She was lovely and would often talk to me about things I didn't know about, but she'd lend me things. She lent me her books, she was so smart, but her mother wouldn't allow her daughter to go to school or college." After a pause, she continued, looking at me with painful and honest earnest. "She knew she was beautiful and she knew she was smart and she knew men would fall in love with her instantly if they were given the chance. She liked being the daughter of a Baron. She loved having a Manor and she loved having servants who waited on her."

Belle sat back in her chair seemingly exacerbated by her statement. It seemed she'd been holding that back for years. It appeared to me if that was the harshest judgement she made of a person, she must have been born with a halo around her head.

"I know exactly the type you mean."

She raised her brows.

"You seem to forget I didn't come from money or class... Well, I did, but that life ended years ago." I stared into the flames, firelight shrouding my face in a red glow as the shadows kicked in to dance on me, thinking of any memory of fire. All I smelt was smoke.

Belle looked at me with a glint in her eye, her face softening. "I hardly knew them, I was so young when I went to the orphanage, about nine or ten they said. I grew up around strangers really."

I turned back to see Belle had shiny eyes, "my mother was treated badly by my father. They weren't married. He used to work here too. He was high upper-class. He used to come and... I guess she couldn't help it. He made her fall for him. That's what she told me. And when she gave herself to him, she never saw him come back. A different man took his place. He was cold and laughed at her when she left rooms, her belly big with me. They said I was lucky they didn't beat me out of her for not being married and for her being so foolish to think he could really love her."

A tear ran down her face, she threw it away quickly.

I held her hand, she didn't look me in the eye, only sniffed and hesitated but ultimately clinging back to my own fingers.

"Sorry, it isn't often I get to talk about it."

My heart ached. She had been stranded at Erlot Manor her whole life; born to it, molded by it and then broken by it. She heard and watched her family scorned and then had her mistress mistreated in front of her; helpless on all accounts but to be simply a part of Erlot's walls.

"Sometimes the only power we have is to listen and remember." I looked at her meaningfully, trying to get her to understand. I was on her side, the same way I was on Meg's.

If Erlot Manor had been polluted by the male mistreatment that permeated its stone walls, that the Winter air desperately crawled inside to wipe away, then I could not let it consume me as well.

"Belle, if anyone, I mean anyone at all, asks about me taking medication, you tell them I take it regularly and it's helping me sleep wonderfully. We are going to go to town now and get me something to replace it in this," I shook the container, "and they won't know we know, okay?"

Chapter 20

MEG

3rd September 1841

Light still glowed on the lawn below my window, darkness inching its way across the countryside. Erlot Manor seemed to darken the first chance it had. The walls oozed shadows and leaked candlewax where the maids had forgotten to snuff the lights out before leaving after dinner.

I sighed as I turned to my room, veins clenching against the icy pit in my stomach. Eyes straying to the shadows that lurked under my bed.

I didn't feel as if I was the only one.

A shudder wracked through me.

I dressed for bed quickly, looking over my shoulder with every movement. Flinching, brushing my hair back swiftly as if the hands would appear in the second it took to slip my nightgown over my head. It fell and hung over my figure, tight around the thighs and brushing my hips. Threads frayed at the end in varying length, brushing my shins. I could not remember when I had gotten it. It had been years. It should have come to the ankles. It had been handed down at the brothel from the older girls. We shared everything, even bath water. Any complaint was matched with the reminder "better in here than out there."

Before I could think it through, I was out of the door. Closing it behind me, my skin almost allergic to the feel of the wood and the brass of the doorknob. I lifted a candle from outside my door and walked softly down the corridor to Rose's door. I waited. My heart fluttered, each pump of blood tickling a rib. I shivered, suddenly feeling naked in that corridor. The light from her room shone under the door.

With one breath, I lifted my hand and knocked.

"Come in."

I bit my lip and turned the doorknob.

There she was at her vanity, brushing her hair. Dark curls twisting in her hands. Dark eyes looked up at me. Wide. Surprised.

I smiled sheepishly, watching her expression change in the mirror.

"I thought you might like my company..." I blushed, pink creeping over my reflection.

Her eyes flashed at me and she turned to view me fully in person. She all but drank me in with her eyes. The deep brown darkening to black.

"Are you scared?" She whispered, lifting herself out of her seat.

I gulped, "not now."

Rose strode towards me. Her figure illuminated through her dress with the candlelight behind her. The windows darkened outside, wind howling. The trees writhed in the distance, a black waving mass like an angry mob outside.

Her hands were like feathers, trailing down my arm to my hands, holding them in her hers. She peered down at them. My eyes followed. Hers were soft and pale, years as a lady had shaped her. But there were white lines. Scars that dotted fingers. My nails had been bitten to the quick. Her fingers danced against mine and I moved forward, lacing them together.

Her head snapped up, eyes meeting mine.

Hesitantly, she leaned forward, soft lips ghosting over my own dry, bitten ones. I breathed in her warm scent. My heart skipped as I moved forward, bridging the gap.

She smiled against my mouth and my knees were weak.

I lay on her chest, our hands, legs and bodies twisted together in one mass of skin that was unrecognisable to the other. Whose hand was whose? Whose leg were whose? Her fingers became mine. Her lips mine and I lay there, warmth surrounding me like a refuge from the nightmares of all the years long before.

After, my blonde her tangled in her dark curls and it made me smile. Her face was flushed, I was sure mine matched, eyes glossed over, shining back at each other, lips red and swollen, sweat glowing on our faces. I nuzzled my face to her chest, trailing feather like kisses up from her breast to her neck. She gasped, her hands drawing lazy circles against my back.

I lay my head back down on her chest, humming happily against her soft skin.

"I have missed you so, my love," she breathed out, her voice quiet and secret. A tone saved only for me. Her other hand found mine and danced with the fingers. I watched them together. "So many years without you…"

"Forget them," I lifted my head, hovering an inch above her face. I hoped my eyes could show a thousand emotions because my heart was pleading with my mind to find the words that escaped me. How can you describe this feeling? How can you explain my love for Rose? The words and language have not been invented.

"All that matters is our time now," I kissed her. She hungrily reciprocated, her hands trailing up my back to cup my cheek. "If you'll have me?" I bit my lip, searching her eyes.

She raised an eyebrow, lips quirking up, "is there any doubt?"

My heart leapt from my chest, straining, as I lay fully against her body, melding together, becoming one for the second time that night.

Her shallow breaths tickled me as she sank into a deep sleep behind me. I felt sleeps' clutches drag me away too, my hands limp in hers our bodies floating together.

A footstep sounded outside the door. I cracked an eye open. A small light loomed through the keyhole. Then footsteps snapped back down the corridor.

Chapter 21

4th December 1837

It felt as though we were sneaking out of the house. The fire may have somewhat dried my hair but the cold clung to any ounce of moisture held by the coils on top of my head, freezing the bun to me like a helmet. My teeth chattered and the grip on my shawl tightened as we walked towards the graveyard on the outskirts of town.

"I know the way," Belle mumbled, as we slowly swung open the little black gate before entering the field of deathly strangers. Each stone stood proud, dropping or wilting with boredom. All a cluster of a past gone by.

"She's just here," she called to me from a little away, stopping by an allotment at the heart of it all.

The Blackwood family plot.

The name Blackwood had been newly inscribed on the place, scratched of the old name hidden by the lick of silver paint. I stood beside her, eyes flickering over the stone.

Here Lies Emily May Blackwood, beloved daughter and sister, taken too soon.

The word 'sister' twisted in my stomach.

One rose had withered away on her soil, shriveled in the cold.

We stood a while just looking at her. I felt a chill run up and down my arms at the thought she was under my feet, looking up at me.

That is when a black figure caught the corner of my eye.

My head snapped up.

It was gone.

I looked behind me.

Nothing but trees and a delicate layer of mist growing stronger with every cold thrash of the wind.

"She never got to leave," Belle whispered.

I looked back at her and took her hand gently in mine, returning my gaze back to Emily Blackwood for Belle's sake. There was no way in Hell they would force me underground surrounded by shadows and fog the way they did Emily.

"Belle, do you remember anything about her father? Is he buried here too?"

I assumed he was dead, but his grave was nowhere to be seen.

"No," she said, "he left years ago. I was very young. So was Emily."

I frowned. How could the Baron leave his home, his wife and children in a cruel cage of ice so quickly? Men could really walk away from all of this?

The black gate creaked in the wind. The air picked up, the mist gliding towards us.

A crow cawed ahead of us, but we couldn't see.

Then a black smudge caught my eye again.

My head snapped round. It was there, whatever it was. Perhaps some other mourners come to pay their respects.

"We should go, it's getting colder," Belle muttered, hand leaving mine as she moved towards the gate. I followed close, afraid I'd lose her in the mist. It was almost like smoke filtering in over the dead and taking them further away from this world. They were now distancing themselves completely from me; more than strangers, more guards to their own, smoke a defence against us intruding. I took one last look at the Blackwood family plot. I could not make out any other names but

Emily's. Except other gravestones of the plot seemed to have surnames beginning with M. Others with A's.

Emily's grave was untouched by the mist and undisturbed by the Winter.

Something sharp tugged my skin.

Searing, the scratch screamed in the icy breeze and oozed blood against the mist.

I gasped, yanking it away, turning to stare at who or what had touched me.

Someone scratched my hand.

No one was there.

I took a closer look.

My hand had a thin scratch across it, oozing droplets of blood on the snow below me.

"Rose," Belle gasped, walking back to me. She looked down at my hand and her eyes grew wide, "are you okay?"

"Something scratched me."

"Did you catch it on the gate?"

She looked over it tenderly, grabbing a napkin from her bag and dabbing at it.

"No, it was-" I bit my lip. I didn't want to sound crazier than I already did. "I don't think it was the gate."

"How peculiar," she tied the napkin around my palm neatly. "Your hands are freezing," she grinned, "we should get you somewhere warm."

In the tearoom we held our cups of tea close to our noses, slouched in our chairs, very disapproving of etiquette. We giggled at ourselves, our bright red noses hovering over the steam, and white fingers gripping it tightly, while our feet melted by the fireside.

We seemed to be the only ones here.

And I much preferred it.

I felt a warmth in my chest that matched memories of me and Meg, like finding daylight peak through the clouds on a dreary day.

"Here are your sandwiches, Miss Blackwood," the waiter announced, placing a plate on the table between us.

"Thank you," I did not correct him.

Belle watched him leave before leaning toward me and whispering, "he must have thought you were Emily!" A look of awe spread over her face quicker than the warmth was doing. "You should have said something."

"She didn't die too long ago, how could the people here forget," I wondered.

Although, if a child died in the orphanage, the staff seemed quick to forget. If a girl was taken away, they put it out their minds. If a boy wandered off, it was not their business.

She thought a while, "well, I suppose two years is long enough. No one knew her very well. She was just one of the Blackwood's. They hardly ever leave here. They come out of Erlot Manor on special business."

My mind flashed back to the other week when George and his mother left to see his lawyer.

"Her death wasn't very public."

I frowned, "I thought that would have been a huge tragedy? A rich *young* woman dead so suddenly."

Belle shook her head, "no, they made a deal to keep it all quiet. They were grieving after all. If I had a daughter or a sister, I don't think I'd appreciate a whole town or newspapers gossiping about it all the time."

I nodded, sipping my tea. The cold had melted away and, after our lunch, we made our way back to Erlot Manor. I had replaced my sedatives with small mints and, upon arriving back at my room, hastily placed them onto my bedside table as if they had never been moved. Belle returned to her own room to get dressed.

I couldn't help but undo the napkin. It clung to my skin, the red stain overtaking the white cotton, slipping away with a net of blood stringing between like a string of saliva. It was pink around the edges and blood still seeped from the gash, black glaring at me from beyond the slit.

What had happened?

Chapter 22

MEG

4th September 1841

Red shone through my eyelids, my arms brushing against something warm and soft.

My eyes fluttered open to see Rose. I shuffled closer until our noses brushed up against each other. My body ached but the sensation was sweet in my muscles, my bones resting happily with hers, as we cradled each other. She was surrounded by her dark hair, coils tied up together like knots of rope. Her dark eyelashes lined her eyes, as they twitched open. Her lips were a pale pink, smooth and parted slightly; her chest moving up and down.

So peaceful.

There was no hint of stiff sadness. She wasn't a statue but a person now.

And suddenly those dark, sparkling eyes popped open to see me.

I felt a pink blush spread across my cheeks, biting my lip as she smiled up at me.

"Good morning," she mumbled, her voice cracking.

I grinned, hands resting under my cheek between the pillow, sleep still blurring my eyes. She was all that was visible. So in focus. The world melted away when her eyes sparkled like that.

"Morning," I breathed, my heart swelled. I do not remember a time where I felt this... content. Like a fire crackled inside me, warming me, keeping me alive but I felt so restful. My mind swam with 'does she feel like this too?'

We remained like that for many minutes, her squirming closer, until her lips were barely against mine like the touch of a ghost. Smoke tickling lungs.

But she pulled back, paling, "we should get ready before anyone notices."

Reluctantly, I pulled myself away and shivered at the cold licking my skin. I scrambled for my nightgown and turned to watch Rose do the same, her face notably flushed when her eyes caught mine.

She giggled and I died.

"Just like old times," I smirked, leaning into her, my hands balanced on the bed post.

"I don't know," she raised an eyebrow, "you never touched me like that before."

It was my turn to blush.

Years had passed and we were not clumsy teenagers. I had been with a few women, other prostitutes for entertainment for the male clients and the rare female client here and there. I wasn't going to show off, but I knew what I was doing.

"You never kissed me like that before."

She smiled, her eyes falling to her hands. The tips of her ears turned red.

"I liked it," I whispered, leaning forward, lifting her chin with the tips of my fingers. I leaned forward, kissing her gently. Coaxing her to not feel embarrassed, let her shyness evaporate under my touch. Guiding an ember to be a fire.

Hands gripped my hips, yanking me forwards, my chest pressed against hers. My heart danced as her tongue licked against my lips, as our bodies melded together like warm candle wax.

Then a knock at the door broke us apart like shattered glass. Wide eyes on wide eyes.

"Just a moment!" Rose called. "Get in there," she nodded to the room with the portraits.

"But-"

"Quick!" Her whisper bit my ears and I dared not argue back. I opened it and closed it in less than a second, way of the click that shocked by insides like lightning. My skin swirled with cold and hot melting against each other, sweat greasing my palm, slipping against the metal of the doorknob. My eyes stared at the door, as I tried to suppress my breathing. It was only going to be the maid but maids gossiped and spread rumours and secrets like wildfire. Although, who was Rose afraid would find out? Her son, her maid, the town?

"Good morning," I could hear the smile in Rose's voice, as she opened the door.

"Hello." It was Anabella.

"Sorry about that, it was so hot in the night, you understand," she was so nonchalant that Baroness should have been scrapped for Lady in those moments. I heard her feet stroll to her vanity, and sit herself down, the maid following close behind.

"I came to see you last night."

Ice to the chest.

"Oh? I was so tired, I fell asleep so quickly, my dear."

A pause.

"I understand."

The silence was deafening. I heard every stroke of hair being brushed.

"Don't be upset," Rose whispered.

"I'm not," Anabella was blunt. "I know how close you two once were."

The brushing stopped.

"This is not that," Rose seemed quieter. As if I was not meant to hear.

I tried to picture them both as they were then. Belle staring at her, hands on her shoulders, on her hair, combing it through. Rose peering shyly at her in the mirror.

I felt sick.

"I hope so."

She finished her hair, helped her dress, and left. All in silence.

When Rose opened the door, I stumbled backwards, blushing as I met her readied self. Dress on, hair up and ready for the day.

"Sorry about that," she muttered, lips twisting the words like a lemon. "She is sensitive to change, and we have this little routine of saying goodnight to each other."

"I did not realise you were so close."

"Oh yes, when I first came here, it was as if I was surrounded by nothing until she became my friend."

I turned to her as I was about to leave. Should I?

"What was that like? When you first came here?"

"Oh," She smiled, but it did not meet her eyes, "I had everything that was promised."

"And... were they part of it?" I nodded toward the room with the portraits. I watched as her lips fells and her eyes narrowed.

"We have discussed this."

I nodded and left.

Chapter 23

ROSE

8th December 1837

I dressed as usual, made sure the pills were strategically placed inside my bedside draw (I was growing suspicious that they check when I'm out). My favourite black boots were laced tightly and ready to brace the snow.

I'd made it a daily habit to escape Erlot Manor with Belle to town or just risk a simple walk in the brisk Winter air. It meant I felt like a walking ice cube when we arrived back, but I was also enjoying our daily sits by the fire, both of us rosy in the face with bright cherry red noses, hot drinks steaming our faces, as our fingers melted, the smell of icy soil permeating our clothing. I felt saner with the cold air filling my lungs a little bit every day. I might suffocate in this room. I think that was his plan.

My boots clicked against the polished mahogany floor as I made my way downstairs. It's so empty here, the hollow echoes away from you and back again. Belle turned, smiling up at me when she saw me coming.

"Ready?"

"Yeah," I smiled, but then I stopped. "George?"

My husband strode towards me, a smile delicately balancing on his thin lips.

Dread flooded my stomach. I was so close to leaving.

His long strides were almost independent from the rest of his body like a spider. His hair had been washed and combed back, his complexion improved, his smile less pathetic than it seemed most evenings. He seemed more of the George I had agreed to marry.

"Darling, where are you off to in such a hurry!" He clapped his hands, looking from me to Belle to me again. "I thought I might take tea with you in the conservatory."

I opened my mouth to argue, but he waved his hand, interrupting me.

"No, no, I know you love the outdoors, but it is *freezing*. I can't have my little wife running off to catch her death."

Belle looked over at me, slowly undoing her bonnet.

I grimaced, "quite right, but I do love the cool air, George. It cleanses the soul and all that."

"I've made arrangement for the conservatory so you will be able to see the garden," he smiled, holding out his arm for me.

My eyes flitted over to Belle for a second. She smiled sadly and made her way back to her room slowly. I sighed, taking his arm.

"I hope it'll be to your liking, my dear."

"Has Matthew been busy, then?" I asked, my voice not disguising any hint of disappointment. I slouched on my way to the conservatory, where the plants were dying, slowly reaching their stalks towards the harsh white sunlight that glared at Erlot Manor every day for only a few hours it could stand being here.

"Yes, did he do well, you think?" He grinned, slipping away to hold out my chair for me. I narrowed my eyes to see through the glass to the outdoors. Mathew had cleared away the snow from the paths, it had melted in puddles in patches in the fields. The flowers and plants had wrinkled and died, but what remained had been dusted off and seemed nice enough. Shrivelled roses drooling icy droplets from their petals.

I nodded, smiling as I sat down, "beautiful."

The servants arrived with our tea, sandwiches and cakes.

"It looks delicious," I beamed at him.

His black eyes glinted back at mine. I looked back down quickly.

The glass house made it colder and I shivered.

"I must ring for Belle to being me my shawl, George." I stated, getting up.

"No need," he held his hand up and nodded at the maid beside us. She scurried away, returning later with a black knitted shawl, with red beads embroidered on the ends.

I held it. Like it could bite me.

"It's very pretty, is it your mothers?" I asked, still seeming to sound sweet. I watched him like a wolf, wary of his every twitch, glint and hesitation. *What are you?*

"No no..." He stared that bright white snow outside, eyes suddenly disinterested in mine.

My normal boldness would have urged to ask if it were Emily's. It was. But, after the night I'd spent with him and asked him a deeply personal question, I felt that was dangerous territory. If Pandora enters the box of chaos, she shouldn't poke it while still inside.

I fling it over my shoulders, the smell of old perfume, dust and time stinging my nostrils. I lowered myself back in my seat.

I poured myself a cup of tea, hesitating over his own cup until a splash of tea hit the bottom of the china and I decided to keep going.

"Don't let it get too cold, now," I warned, eyes catching his and smiling back.

"Wouldn't dream of it," he winked, adding the milk and sipping it, humming against the rim. I had a flashback still of his lips against mine and I almost choked on my tea. I tried to keep the shudder to myself. His clammy hands cradling the cup with his long bony fingers.

"I always forget you take yours so... un-feminine," he nodded at my own cup.

I bit back a frown, "I see you use sugar..." I hid a smile in another sip.

His eyes looked between mine.

After meaningless chat about the weather, he eyed me slowly before asking, "how have you been sleeping?"

"Very well, those pills your mother gave me send me off like a light."

"I'm glad. I was worried you were becoming... restless in the night."

I smiled, "oh no, especially not now." I grinned, "it's almost as if I'm dead each night."

It was then the air grew colder, harsher on the lips and eyes.

And I knew his mother entered the room.

"Mrs. Blackwood," I smiled, accidentally slamming my cup on the saucer, splashing tea all over the table. The maid lurched forward with a napkin.

"It's Ms actually," she pressed her grey lips into a thing line as I fell over myself apologising to both her and the maid alike, almost grabbing the napkin to clean it up myself, who very urgently and politely gripped it like a vice.

"Mrs Blackwood..."

I looked up, the Baroness fixed me with a hard stare, almost bored by the matter at hand.

"Yes,... Ms?" I said sweetly, slowly sitting down in my chair, eyes never leaving hers. "Oh," I squeaked, "do join us, there's plenty tea and sandwh-"

"No, I'm quite alright," she narrowed her eyes. "Perhaps you should slow down, though. Don't want to be too full for dinner."

"Oh," I flushed, "I get so tired and weak by dinner time, you see. Those pills put me in quite a daze, but they do work awfully well, I have to say!"

Her eyes flashed.

"Glad to hear it. We've been so worried about your sleeping habits, we thought you'd never settle down here."

It was the most words that had poured out of her mouth in one go, I was surprised at how her voice sounded. It wasn't croaky or too stern or deep as it usually was in her short curt answers to me before. There was a hint of a human being behind that voice.

"Yes," I hesitated, "thank you again for the pills, they've really changed my life." My eyes flickered like a candle towards George.

He changed around his mother, his face bent down slightly, hands in front of his lap and sat upright, legs together like a good schoolboy. It was strange to see him change so suddenly, he seemed to want to be free with me, but now a canary trapped in a cage.

No, not a canary. A fly who had made a pact with the spider.

Chapter 24

MEG

8th September 1841

There I found myself, with a soft breeze brushing my hair back for me like a lover, hot coffee spreading through my stomach, hands clamming up. The days seemed ever-changing. The sun shone for now, though. A bite of chill in the air, though. I walked aimlessly, deciding to explore the grounds further. In the weeks I'd been here, I'd stayed with the garden, having been wary of Rose's approval and the gardener who kept watching us. The maid was nowhere to be seen and Rose was having to look over her finances for the day. Lady of the house.

The grass was scorched ahead of me, brown and patchy, withering next to its green cousin, that darkened in the shadow of the forest that engulfed the grounds. I wandered towards them, stopping when I heard a gasp from behind me. I turned to see a sheepish and flushed Leopold Blackwood. Dark hair shining in the sun, messy from where his hand could not stop brushing it. In fact, when he caught my eye, he brought a small pale hand to tangle into it, taking a deep breath. He was like a bashful young man in that moment, then his eyes met mine and he was a child again. I turned fully to him.

"You look like a boy who's up to no good."

He looked at his feet, hand trailing to rub the back of his neck. His dark brows knitted together, his eyes searching for words.

My lips quirked, "do you want to tell me? I promise I can keep a secret."

"Well," his eyes looked anywhere but mine. "I was just drawing..."

I smiled, kneeling next to him, "can I see?"

He shuffled back down to the ground, cross-legged next to me, handing me a piece of paper slowly. I took it carefully, as if were made of glass and let my eyes wander over the detailed pencil strokes. The outlines were wobbly, and the boy had trouble shading, but for a five-year-old he was talented.

"This is very good," I looked over at him. Blush spread across his cheeks. He blushed the same way his mother did. A delightful dash of pink they shared. I smiled.

"Why did you try to hide this?"

"Oh, mother says art is a sin."

I flinched, frowning down at the ground. "What?" I thought he was pulling my leg with that one. Rose was never very strongly religious. I mean, how can you be when the same people preaching celibacy are visiting you every night.

He gulped, letting out a sigh, resting his chin on his fist, playing with the paper idly.

"She says only bad people become artists and that if I paint or draw it's the devil speaking through me. She made Belle take me to church once and they all said the same thing. Oh, and she also says artists are liars and deviants, but I don't know what that means."

"Did she say that to you?"

He nodded, ears turning red.

"I see. Spying, are we?"

He looked down.

I glanced up at him. Was he lying? Why would a child lie? He must be kidding, pulling a prank on me, some little boys love to do that. That was not the Rose I knew and loved.

"So art's terrible, huh?" I was at a loss for words. They stirred in my chest, along with the icy sensation of confusion. Rose believed art was a sin?

I felt my heart sting with what she must think of me. If art was a sin, what was sex? What was prostitution? Had she forgotten what we were?

"Yeah, but I don't feel like a bad person when I do it..." He frowned at the grass. I followed his eyes.

"No, I don't think you are at all."

There was a pause.

"How long are you here for?"

I jumped, turning to face him. "I don't know."

"Mother says you were friends when you were little?"

"Yes."

"How come I never met you before?"

"Perhaps you did," I raised an eyebrow, "you just don't remember."

"I don't forget too easily," he shook his head. "Mother does."

"What does she forget?" My voice grew quieter.

"Well," he paused, glancing up at me for a moment. He took a moment before continuing. For a five-year-old, he was very intelligent, I thought. I could see Rose in him, but I had never met or seen his father. Did Rose see her husband in him?

"Well, mother keeps visiting me in the night sometimes. Belle said maybe she sleepwalks. But mother said she doesn't."

"She visits you?"

"Yeah, but she doesn't remember."

I frowned, paling. "Does she seem different at night?"

He looked at me. Silence.

I took out a cigarette and lit it, the cold air getting stuffy.

"What did your father think of your art?"

"I don't know."

I bit my cheek as ice flooded my veins. How could I forget that? What an idiot.

I glanced to the sky, hoping God got a chuckle out of my pitiful life.

My head turned back to look at Erlot for a second. My eyes catching a shadow in the attic window.

I squinted, heart stopping.

Dark hair, pale complexion, feminine silhouette.

It must be Rose.

Did she always have to watch her son? Was I even allowed near him?

It felt like me and Leo had a secret club away from the people of Erlot in that moment. Discussing everything swept under the rug. A five-year-old was more honest with me in those moments than I could hope for from Rose in months. It was refreshing but the guilt lingered in my chest.

"Leopold!"

We both turned sharply to see Anabella storming towards us, wringing her hands.

"I have to go!" Leo looked at me quickly, scrambling to stand up.

"Oh, Leo, you've got dirt all over your shorts!" Annabella looked him up and down, holding him by the shoulder. She sighed, exasperated, hair falling from the pins holding it in place. Each strand of hair loose floated in the wind and tickles her shoulders. Her rounds eyes looked down on him and softened. "It's okay though, we'll get you cleaned up before dinner."

I stood up, dusting off my skirt.

She looked over at me, her eyes hardening into a stern stare.

I kept her gaze as I took a drag.

"Leo go on inside, and get Maria to draw you a bath."

"But-"

"Your mother wants you cleaned up for dinner."

"That's hours away, though!"

"Plenty of time to go get ready, then, isn't it?"

With a huff, the little boy trudged back towards the Manor, having shoved his drawing under his shirt. His hands held the hem, making it a bit too obvious he was up to something.

I raised an eyebrow as the maid looked me up and down.

"The weather is changing," she sighed. "I sense it will be getting a lot colder soon."

"It was warm this morning."

"It would be for you," she mumbled.

"I don't mind, I like a cold Winter."

"Isn't that convenient."

There was silence between us, and I took a drag, smoke curling in my throat. The wind had become chillier, nipping at my skin. My nose and ears were always the first to feel it.

"Perhaps, you better find somewhere for the Winter months. The London smog can be so warming, I hear."

I glanced at her, we were both watching the trees ahead of us. I felt like nature had become my audience for this awkward stand-off.

"I don't plan to see London for a while, it won't miss me too dearly,"

"Is that so? Erlot Manor can be icy come December. We struggle to get warm."

"I am sure I will manage."

"I have noticed that your type is quite adept at finding ways to keep warm... I suppose body heat is one way to survive the Winter."

I let out a chuckle with a clenched jaw, eyes straight ahead. Did everyone here know?

"I don't quite understand your meaning, but I have observed that, if it truly becomes unbearably cold, those who cling to loneliness die first."

I blew smoke at her cheek.

She bit back a choke.

I could feel the red rise up her neck. Her fists clenched at her sides. I turned my gaze back to the trees, a smirk resting on my lips.

"I am aware of your other inclinations towards my mistress," she whispered in my ear like it was poison on her lips.

"Oh," I smirked. "Are you also aware that me and your *mistress* share the same history."

She was silent. I turned to catch her eyes. Doe eyes burning into mine. Light fading out.

"Rose could survive the coldest Winters... whereas you..." I waved my hand at her, biting back a grin as I watched her shake with anger. With one look toward the trees, the maid stormed off back to Erlot Manor.

Immediately, my stomach swelled with an empty pit burrowing deeper into me. What had I just done?

Given Rose more reason to want me gone again.

Chapter 25

ROSE

9th December 1837

The next day he stopped me leaving the house by insisting I study his painting for any mistakes.

Paint splattered the sheets strewn all over the floor. The candles flickered in the harsh winter sunlight at the room. Paint was blobbed over palettes, colours curling into one another, lurching forward into contrast and warming to harmonious brothers and sisters beside them. His paint was at war with itself and the portrait in front of me had a similar effect on my mind.

"Do you like it?" He asked, almost breathless, dark eyes looming from me to the painting.

It was of me, but it was not me.

I stared at her and she stared back. Threat ran from the black paint of her eyes and poisoned my own. Dark hair almost disappeared into the black background that surrounded me, the curls hanging around my face tightly, so precisely placed in a frame around my forehead and pinned tightly on top. Not at all like the accidental fluff that flopped out of my buns every day. Curls that escaped and had a life of their own; these were meticulous... mechanic.

The tight corset strangled my waistline and pushed my breasts obscenely high and plump. The dark grey gown that flowed over my body was not mine. The dark red ruby necklace was subtly painted around my neck.

And those eyes. They were meek and knowing at once. I couldn't tell from looking at the painting, if this was the me I had never met or the me I had never wanted to face. It struck the air out of my lungs how closely I resembled his sister. A shade lighter hair, slightly more flecks of yellow in the eyes, stronger eyebrows, not quite as pale as her rich skin had allowed her.

In fact, I felt that, with every brush stroke, he had strived to make me more like Emily.

"It's beautiful," I whispered, eyes never leaving the paint. "I don't think I've ever worn that dress... or that necklace?"

I turned to find him watching me, looming over me from afar. His dark eyes like black holes; something inside finding me. Alone. In his studio.

"No, but that is my next little present," he smiled, holding up his hand for me to wait there as he excitedly wondered off. I felt dread churn in my stomach, like a restless bat in a lonely cave, desperate to leave.

He traipsed back inside the studio, a silver dress draped over one arm and, held cautiously in two hands, the ruby necklace from the painting. I turned slowly, the hairs raising warily on my neck as his hands ghosted over the skin and laid the necklace on my chest. I watched the rubies rise and fall with every breath as he clasped it around my neck. Was this a mark on my grave?

The red contrasted with the pale blue dress I'd decided on that day. Angrily sitting there, the righteousness surging in the blood red sparkle of each gem, a smirk hidden behind each one, as I turned back to my husband and smiled.

"Oh, George," I glittered my eyes at him, "they're beautiful!" I beamed. I pressed my hand gently on his arm, forcing sunlight to burst through my eyes as I saw my reflection beaming back at me in those pitiful dark eyes.

I leaned forward and pressed my lips to his.

It was quick but married us again in that moment.

"Shall I try on the dress, or do you wish me to wear it to dinner tonight?"

His lips spread, revealing his teeth.

"You would look lovely tonight," he took my hand in his. He looked down at it and caressed my small fingers with his thumb. It was a foreign sensation. This was the romantic George from the proposal, a bright contrast to the wedding night version that leapt from him like a werewolf in the full moon. "And you must wear the rubies. My mother insists on you being at dinner tonight, and I have to say, I have missed your presence. After all," he dropped my hand, "what is the point in having a wife if you don't see her." He handed me the dress. He didn't mention the faded red scratch on my palm, that winced at the sight of the rubies.

When I was back in my room, I caught my reflection in the mirror. I slowly watched my hand creep up my torso to the rubies, twisting one in the light. The red around my neck felt strange and I felt it choking me, weighing me down. Disgust suddenly tore through my body, lips twisting like I'd eaten a lemon, and I quickly unclasped the necklace and threw it down on the bed.

I felt its presence burn into my neck and I watched the mirror for any sign of Emily. Or the me I once knew for that matter. What was I to be? His wife or his victim? It was as if no one in the whole of Erlot Manor knew, but we were all waiting patiently for Fate to show us.

The dress rested on my bed ready to be worn. I had a horrible shudder repress itself inside me, whispering in my mind that this belonged to Emily.

Perhaps Fate had already decided, and it was to be his sister.

And, as I have missed two months of bleeding, a mother too.

Chapter 26

MEG

8th September 1841

I strode towards the forest, feeling fire simmer the blood that rushed to my face. The cool wind stung my ears and burned my eyes. My jaw ached from clenching, grinding my teeth as I mulled over the maid's words.

How dare she talk to me like that? Was I lower than the maid here? Was I a guest? What was I here? What was I to Rose?

Was I the mistress to the Lady of the house? If so, did that mean I had the upper hand? I bit my lip, staring at the darkened trees before me.

I supposed it did. I let the poison spread a warmth through my veins, the shadows that surrounded me cooled my blood and the thoughts of entering Erlot Manor again curdled my stomach acid. I shivered, looking around at the house. It felt too close and yet too far away. These grounds were vast and could easily lose you. The forest whispered to me and I wandered forward, anger had let me forward. Copper slid onto my tongue and I stopped biting my lip.

What was that?

Just beyond the edge of the trees was a small stone in the ground like a grave. I moved forward, only a step into the forest, and I already felt cut off from Erlot Manor. I was in another world. A world of surroundings that leered and whispered to themselves. Twigs cracked like broken bones under my heel, leaves squelched into the mud like bodies in battle.

It was a gravestone. I bent down to inspect, brushing the leaves that hand piled up in front. A grey, cracked stone had been forced into the ground, dead flowers from long ago scattered the floor around it. I scratched at the moss, uncovering a name.

George Blackwood.

I frowned, clawing at the dirt underneath to fine just one date: 1835.

I sat back on my heels; shoulders slouched as I took it in. The headstone stared back at me. And, as if the body that lay beneath me had shivered, I shook myself quickly and bounced backwards on my back in realisation. There was something horrible about kneeling on someone's grave. Only a few feet of dirt lay between me and a corpse. I shuddered, hands shaking at the thought. Why was there a grave all the way out here?

Rose had mentioned in one of her letter's years ago that her husband and her mother-in-law had had a proper funeral in the graveyard in town. Who was this then? Why would she bury him out here? I was sure her husband was named George... but he died 1837.

Unless this was some secret first child? No, I shook my head, they were not married until Early November 1837.

The memory of her words rang bitterly inside my head, echoing, taunting me. Not only did she leave. But she left with him. For here. The one person I felt I could survive it all for left me behind in her dust. She raised herself up into a cloud, practically floating above the dirty and alcohol filled life of mine.

She became a Baroness with a name and maids. I stayed a dirty prostitute who longed, aching, for her to come back and take me away. Is that how she looked at me now? Tears sprang into my eyes and I gasped a sob at thoughts uninvited. Not now, I breathed slowly, squeezing my eyes shut. Holding a breath, I willed the ache to die away. Slip away like sunset. I felt my skin crawl with calloused hands, with eyes. Who knew eyes could hurt you?

I bit my lip, drawing blood. Salty tears and copper filled my mouth, and I shook my head at how pathetic I must seem to anyone watching. The ground before me felt soft under my hands. I refused to open my eyes. Simply bent forward on the dirt, hands caked in soil, nails bitten by moss from the grave, eyes streaming reluctant tears, mouth bitten red, and choking on sob after sob.

Finally, it subsided. A weight lifted from my shoulders and my body stopped hiccupping sobs. I stopped biting down on my lip, the cool air stinging the blood there. I took a shaky breath, opening my eyes. My hands released the dirt I'd clenched tightly in both fists. Gulping down another breath, I looked up. Then I reached out to touch the gravestone. As my hand rested on the name, dirty hands marring the words, I felt an emptiness stretch out inside my stomach. It spread through me the way warmth washes over you in a hot bath. Slowly and yet suddenly. I shivered as it wrapped around my ribs and up through my neck. My lips felt like two ice cubes, cheekbones aching and eyes frozen with droplets of tears like morning dew on ivy leaves. It was if I had not cried before. As if I could not feel the pain of those words and memories. They had lost their sting. In fact, I could not feel. I was numb.

My head turned to see Erlot Manor watching me. More specifically, a figure was. The mist had seeped from the forest and had floated toward the Manor, swirling around its crumbling rocks. The lights in the windows illuminated each room. The warmth of it shaking the trees around me in envy. Rose watched me. Her dark silhouette in my window. Why was she in my room?

I wiped my eyes with my hands. But the moment I touched my face I groaned as I smeared dirt across my eyes. I wiped hastily with the sleeves of my dress, dirtying the dress Rose had leant me earlier. I sighed, picking myself up off the floor and brushing off the leaves. I felt numb and dirty.

Did she see me?

With one last look at the grave, I walked forward. The hair on the back of my neck stood on end as I turned my back. Twigs and leaves rustled behind me but I trained my eyes on the window that watched me. As I moved closer to Erlot Manor, she disappeared.

Then I heard shuffling.

There was a long wall ahead and a small nook before the drawing room window.

I leant back and squinted.

There was a man there, peering into the window.

Shrouded in shadow.

I felt my heart stop.

Breathe, Meg, breathe.

I waited a second. Frozen to the spot. He took a swig from a bottle in his hand. As he turned to drink, he noticed me and froze. It was Mathew the gardener. My heart beat again but my breathing was wary of his presence. No one could see me easily from this position and he was drinking. I clutched the brass button in my pocket.

"What do we have here?" He smiled, stumbling away from the wall.

I raised an eyebrow.

"Were you spying on someone?"

He chuckled, but then hiccupped at the same time so it was to tell.

"Just checking on the Missus."

"Aren't you a gardener?"

He took another swig from his bottle. His eyes stared at me, looking me up and down.

I shuffled under his gaze.

As the sun went down, it cast an orange glow across his cheeks. His eyes were hard to make out, but I could see his blonde hair poke out from his cap. His clothes were fraying, and he brought his hand up to wipe his lips. It seemed a bit exaggerated and I dared not laugh.

"I thought so," he muttered, "but I don't have half as much dirt on me as you do."

I flushed, hoping to God he couldn't see in this light.

"I tripped," I tried. My voice faltered, and my eyes flitted briefly to his bottle and then back to his eyes. He smiled.

My breathing slowed at the realisation he was just some drunken gardener outside. He was not a threat to me.

His toothy grin watched me for a moment before he shuffled his feet and almost stumbled to the ground. I smirked and shook my head, stepping away to head in.

"Wait!" He slurred. "You aren't going to say anything, are you?"

His eyes pled with me, but his smile was leering.

"Why? You were only just checking on her." I feigned innocence, taking a step backwards toward the entrance.

"Yeah, got to keep your wits about you, you see." He stumbled forwards towards me and I took several more steps back.

"Definitely, with a voyeur around," I smirked.

"I was not-" He looked at me, taking a deep breath and then puffing it back out, the smell of alcohol washed my voice and I winced. "Just making sure she's where she is, you know."

I frowned, "you're not making any sense, I think you need to stop," I waved at the bottle in his hand, "that."

"Nah, I need my medicine," he said seriously. I huffed out a laugh at that.

"Well, I'm going inside. I hope Rose is where she should be," I roll my eyes, about to leave, yet again.

He lunged forward, taking my arm. I squirmed away, slapping his hand. He released me quickly. Looking me dead in the eyes.

"How well do you know her?"

"What?" I wanted nothing more but to leave. I felt the hands on me again like burns or bruises.

"Do you think you know her?"

"Yes," my voice caught in my throat.

He grinned, "okay."

He turned and left me then. Swaying away into the distance. As I turned to go inside, I heard him mutter under his breath "skeletons... closets."

The people here are almost as strange as the nights.

Chapter 27

10th December 1837

That night at dinner wearing the dark silver dress, that hugged my ribs like the plague and rustled with every movement I made like the chains of a prisoner. The ruby necklace burned against my chest and choked my neck. Nonetheless I beamed sweetly at my family as I bid them a good evening.

"George tells me he has been painting you, have you seen his work yet, Mrs. Blackwood?" The Baroness asked, skewering some bird's flesh on her fork before popping it into her mouth. I winced, looking down at my own meal. I suddenly did not feel hungry, dreading the night ahead.

"I have, yes," I mumbled, deciding to sip my wine instead. "It's very George."

"Very George? What does that mean, George? Is it your style or is she trying to be witty?"

He simply smiled, "perhaps she is doing both."

"No, I never joke when it comes to art," I swirled the wine in the glass, watching the red liquid race around the cup and never daring to spill it. "That would be completely wicked, especially in front of the painter." I bit back the smile I was hiding.

"Ah, but to like all art is to be naïve, is it not?" His eyes watched me as I decided to try a bite, hoping the twists in my stomach would allow it.

"Yes, but I find we don't have to be too cruel to things we dislike."

The Baroness raised her eyebrows, "do you find people are often cruel to things they dislike, Mrs Blackwood?"

"Oh," I almost choked as the meat slid down my throat. If only they knew. "I think it is human nature to want to destroy something we see as a threat to our own happiness. Having something in our life we dislike does just this, but," I took another sip of wine, "I've found that women are more sensible in those fields. Men destroy what they dislike *and* what they love."

"Oh, very wicked, indeed," George muttered, losing interest or seemingly uncomfortable. The Baroness raised an eyebrow, smirking.

"I do find that women who say such things about men are never heard of again."

I flushed and went back to the wrestle with my dinner and my stomach.

Before I left, I summoned the courage.

I told them I was with child. And that a new Blackwood would be born for them.

I don't know what I was expecting, but the Baroness stared at me, her wine glass half-way to her lips. George paled but his smile stretched across his skull, a twinkle in his eye.

"I am going to be a father," he whispered.

Once dinner had finished, I said good night to my husband and mother-in-law, and slowly made my way back to my room, ringing the bell for Belle as soon as I entered the room. I unclasped the ruby necklace and dropped it on the floor, and sat on my bed, head in my hands. I was playing with fire and forgot I was not part of the embers.

"Rose," Belle whispered as she opened the door. "How was dinner?" She eyed me. I knew she was specifically wanting to know how they took the news.

I turned for her to undo my dress, mulling over my answer carefully. "Manageable."

"I think people started to talk about you in town, I was thinking that might be why he keeps you here now."

"Why would that-" I frowned.

"You look like her," she whispered fiercely. "You need to remember that."

I stepped out of my dress, stark white corset and bloomers emerging from the dark silver atrocities he'd tied me to.

"He painted me," I muttered, gaging her reaction. "Do you want to see?"

After throwing on my robe, we waited a few hours, wasting time playing cards by the fire, until we were sure George and the Baroness would be in bed. I took the lead, as we softly padded to the studio, I kept turning to hold a finger to my lips when she'd slip on the polished wood. We made the decision to walk about in our stockings so as to not wake anyone. Which meant the floorboards became our enemy for the night, not just the darkness that permeated Erlot Manor when the sun left it.

"Here," I whispered under my breath, pointing to a door. I handed her my candle, and turned the door, praying he had not locked it.

He had not. It swung open slowly, revealing the paint and the mess I had witness earlier that day.

We filtered in, slowly clicking the door shut behind us. There was something exciting about sneaking around together, we tried not to giggle like children. All smiles ceased when we looked at the portrait.

There I was, meek, small, dark and ghostly.

"It doesn't.... it looks like you," she muttered. "But, it doesn't feel like you."

"No," I breathed. I knew what she meant. I felt it the first time I'd stared into those dark eyes. Hollow but scared.

"Isn't art meant to imitate life?"

"No," I sighed. "Art imitates the artist's perspective on life."

She looked back at the portrait with me with wide eyes, "so this is his perspective of you."

I nodded, paling, "this is how he sees me."

She scrunched her nose up in disgust, "he sees a scared Emily..."

I bit my lip, "I've started to think perhaps the portraits of her... the nude one, especially, are his own perspective...."

She looked down, "I didn't know very much about it, but, they were a pretty messed up pair together."

I nodded, clasping my hand in hers. We gripped each other and watched my portrait all night, almost hoping we'd find more remnants of me in there. A fragment of myself stowed away under all the façade he'd filled the canvas with.

I was some meek look-alike to him, and nothing more. I was right in thinking I was just a body to him.

"This works in my favour," I breathed, turning to meet Belle' large blue eyes. "If he doesn't see who I am, he won't know what's going to happen."

Chapter 28

MEG

8th September 1841

The walls are bare.

I walked into Erlot Manor and it had only just struck me properly how bare it all was. The dim flickering candles cast shadows all around me. The bare walls groaned as the fog lapped at the outside of its skin. Every wall was just a wall. Upper class houses were meant to have their ancestors painted on every surface, weren't they? I should have been stared down by Erlot himself. I shivered. I didn't feel there needed to be physical eyes painted everywhere for me to feel watched. The house would loom over me, as I wandered room to room, eyes trailing along the stonework.

Then I saw Belle ahead of me, towels in hand.

"Sorry, Miss," my throat cracked. I tried to look ahead at the wall and not in her eyes. They were probably red and puffy. I shuddered to think she would think it was about her and her words earlier.

She turned on her foot, and I narrowly dodged a venomous stare, instead it bored away into my temple from a far.

"Yes?" She huffed out, fiddling with the pile of towels in her hands.

"I know that these stately homes, with centuries of history behind them, usually have a fond nature of preserving those memories." I raised an eyebrow, but kept my face hidden by shadow. "Usually, portraits of everyone that so much as sneezed on the grounds are hung in every room, but Erlot Manor seems to neglect this... why are there no paintings at all?"

"There are some–"

"No, every room has none. I have looked and I have only just realised it. This is such a bare house."

She sighed, taking a moment to watch me. I had the feeling, without needing to look at her, that I was treading a tightrope with her. I had already implied her beloved mistress had been a prostitute and now I was interfering with the décor. Those doe eyes homed in on my skull and she mulled over her words.

"They burned in the fire."

I nodded. It made sense. Until it didn't.

"Even the ones in the rooms the fire didn't reach?"

As far as I knew and could tell from the odd brickwork of Erlot Manor, the fire had managed to be contained. Only a few rooms had been engulfed and burned to the ground.

"There weren't many paintings to begin with."

"I thought Mr Blackwood was a painter?"

"He was also a very private man."

"So private as to conveniently have the rooms on fire be the only rooms to contain his work?"

Silence.

"Is that all, Miss Marrilow?"

I thought it over, taking my time, letting her smoke a little in anger. She clicked her tongue at me, and my lips quirked up.

"Yes, I suppose, thank you."

Chapter 29

21st January 1838

I'm starting to show now.

The pills they were giving me suddenly disappeared from my room the day after I told them all the news. The doctor comes now and then to reassure me everything's normal, but I don't like him, he's the Blackwood's family doctor. I don't need to see him as often I do. I could sneeze and he suddenly appears.

He always does house visits too. Only.

Since the announcement it's been George's new excuse to keep me in this prison. I don't so much mind for now, but there's a hole in my stomach that widens and shudders at night when I think what will happen after all this. For now this thing growing inside me seems to make me the family favourite. I am the vessel of an heir and therefore precious. Will they poison me again after I give them a new heir? If it's a boy, mostly likely. If it's a girl, they'll keep me around. At least that's what I'm convinced on.

What Belle said still rings in my head in those dark nights, when it is just me and my mind playing tricks. The breeze tickles the curtains, the moon casts an icy glow over my room. I sit up in bed rubbing circles on my womb. I can feel them in there. So small and tiny but full of life. Not quite bursting with the energy to be known but my blood is alive with the knowledge I am not alone anymore.

But if it is a girl, I am still replaceable.

Emily wasn't kept around.

Chapter 30

MEG

9th September 1841

The door shut behind me with a click. The air was stuffy, and the window was locked shut. The dwindling orange glow of the sun faded away until a deep violet hue dusted the room. Rose watched me through her mirror, eyes glancing up now and then, faded whenever they landed on herself.

"Why do you keep yourself here like a museum piece?" I sighed, staring ahead, back against the door. I breathed slowly, letting my eyes flutter towards her. I felt the day on my shoulders pushing me and my knees wobbled.

She frowned, looking at herself, as she fussed with her hair. "What do you mean? I live here."

I huffed, flinging myself upright and sliding my arms around her bed post, vaguely staring out the window. "We have never once gone to town since I have arrived."

"I am enjoying your company." There was that doll-like smile. Rehearsed. Wifely.

"You have been enjoying it for over a month. Without leaving the house. In fact, you hardly go in the garden..."

I swung round on the bedpost like a child, the wood squeaking against my palms.

"Do you expect to be me to be parading about now I'm a Lady?"

"I just wondered," I shrugged. I lay down on her bed in a dramatic sigh. "I'm not complaining, but don't you *need* air?"

I bit my lip, fingers tingling with embarrassment.

I heard her stool creak and I did not need to look up to know she had turned to see me fully.

She giggled, "no, I seem to be managing fine without."

"I just worry about you," I breathed. The world drifted by as she made me wait. I held my breath. Did not dare to look up. My hand tingled for my brass button out of habit, though. The silences always ate at me. It was poisonous, sinking into you slowly and killing you without knowing it. Then, years later you find yourself deathly afraid of something non-lethal. The worst weapon.

She leaned over me. I flinched.

Her eyes scanned my face, her hands were white as they gripped the bed post.

Her breath brushed over my lips, and I shivered. Her eyes, though, were dark and cold. When her lips quirked into a smile, they shifted to starlight and a shudder spiralled down my spine like lightning. I felt numb spread through me. My fingers like ice made her flinch from me. She straightened up and raised an eyebrow.

"You're as cold as death."

"Thank you," I rolled my eyes. "If we're dealing comparisons, you are as a blunt as a spoon."

She shook her head, eyes lighting up again.

"Ha. Ha. And you have all the manners of a starved raccoon."

"And you have all the wit of a toddler."

There was a knock at the door.

"Rose, Leo has called for you," Belle interrupted.

"I'll be down in a bit!"

"And she has all the humour of a corpse."

I grumbled. I could still feel the cold travel through me in waves, like ice pulsating in my veins. I shivered and closed my eyes, pinching the bridge of my nose.

"I think I'm not well."

"What's wrong?" Rose leaned forward and felt my forehead. Gasping, she drew back. "You're like ice!"

"I know," I looked at my hands.

"Maybe... you should rest early," Rose held her hand out, and I took it, standing up felt like a chore. My legs were numbing out, and I wobbled unsteadily on my feet. She helped me out of the door and across the way to my room. I pushed the thoughts of the hands from my head. Rose kissed my cheeks, hissing at the cold of my skin, before turning to unlace my dress, slowly pushing it down to my ankles for me to step out of. I watched the room, trying not to linger on one spot too much. I shivered, my stomach convulsed and a whoosh of cold liquid bubbled inside me. I groaned, climbing into my bed, the sheets covered me, and I watched Rose's face come into view.

Dark eyes. They were hazel really, but you could only tell when the sun caught them just right. Like it could shine through her and show you all her colours. But the rest of the time it was hard to tell. Bit brown eyes that tried to analyse you. Inquisitive and watchful like a hawk. I shivered as they bored into me. I did not mind; it wasn't like that maid's stare. There was a fire in those. The thought of fire only made the cold thrash angrily inside me. My head ached; it took feeling icy. My eyes fluttered.

"You'll feel better in the morning," she cooed softly. I smiled weakly back.

Her hair was also more of a dark brown than a black. But in the dark now it was like angry shadows flicking around her chest in taunting curls. Her face was round and dewy, too, but the years and made her pale and gaunt. There were glimpses in her smile of youth, though.

She faded from me, and I was floating. The world travelled passed my eyelids, I felt like I was falling, my body tried to clench against the bed, as my stomach lurched with the motions of light that dodged my eyeballs. I could not focus on any one colour that flitted past. I could not scream. My throat was not there. It was not choked up or strangled. It did not belong to me. I had no voice to cry out or scream with. I felt my mind groan for me and then I opened my eyes.

Dark eyes watched me from above. Rose?

The world was blurry. I blinked.

Dark hair. Black hair and black eyes. Not Rose.

I felt frozen to my bed, sweat dripped from my forehead, tickling my hairline as it trailed down my skin. Shaky breaths shivered in my lungs, and it took me a while to realise I was shaking.

She stared at me. Numb coldness piercing into me. Her skin was grey, almost translucent, and her eyes were round and glassy with sorrow. I choked, trying to find my voice. Thoughts of her lashing out suddenly flooded my mind. She was so still I was pinned to the bed.

Cold hands pressed on mine.

I could have screamed. Kicked. Yelled for help.

I was glued to my bed. My body did not dare twitch. Those eyes never once blinked. Completely focused on me. The rest of her seemed to fade away, as my head rushed to keep me awake.

Her hands were like water, silky, slippery, and almost not there. Like I was in a horrible dream. Then I blinked and her face opened wide and she screamed.

"Meg!"

I was crying, sobs wracking my body, my entire body violently shaking.

"Meg, it's okay, hey," Rose's voice was in my ear. Soft and silky.

Her hair tickled my cheek, and I drenched each curl in tears.

"Shhh, I'm here," she held me tightly like I would slip away suddenly. I held on just as tight. I felt like I was spinning again. Like if she let go, I'd fade away.

When the sobs subsided, I breathed slowly in and out. She placed my cold hands on her chest to urge me to keep going. I breathed as best I could. My lungs felt empty and full at the same time. I nuzzled my face into her neck and tried inhaling her scent instead. Her warm skin. Her soft touches to my head. I realised she was still whispering things into my ear. MY arms had somehow found their way around her waist. I could feel her ribs and her spine. The lavender and cotton filled my lungs. My sweat dripped onto her. Our smell mingled together, and I felt myself come back down to Earth.

"Thank you," I mumbled weakly.

She laid me back down. I felt like a sack of potatoes. As I drifted back to sleep, Rose clambered over me and held me, her light fingers combing through my hair.

I hummed peacefully, "Thank you."

Chapter 31

ROSE

6th March 1838

The life inside my womb keeps growing. I catch myself staring at the swelling in the bath. Bobbing above the surface of the water. I stare at it and think you're a living thing.

Inside me.

He grows stronger every day and it scares me. I feel he's a boy. I made Belle hold a pendulum over my belly, the same way Akwete used to do back. If he is a boy, ... I'm terrified he'll be like George. How much are children like their fathers really, though? Am I like my mother? Impossible for me to know, but how likely could it be?

I'm kept inside like a glass doll now. It's funny how I ache to go somewhere. Anywhere. I feel so disconnected from the world. It's spinning away from me and I'm fading into the grey stones of Erlot. All I see are the grey stones, the trees, the fields. All I have is Erlot, and it is not welcomed to me. My child is still mine, and no one else can touch him yet. He doesn't feel the chill in the air, the shadows that reach toward me at night, the cries of another woman's baby in the mornings. He never has to know.

At least I have Belle, but I can't stand seeing the same reflection, the same fire, the same walls. The same grey permeates the fields around Erlot Manor and no matter how long you stare out the windows they don't change.

Chapter 32

MEG

9th September 1841

My hands still shook the next morning. I fumbled with my dress and hair and felt my eyes freeze open at the memories of last night. Was it a bad dream? It felt real. My body shuddered. Her hands were cold on mine. My hands felt like hers. Each groove of her fingertip that slid over my arm made vomit curdle in my throat.

I shook my head, loosely making a grasp for my button in my pocket, but I only brushed over it. The sensation breaking through the numb.

Rose kept shooting me worried glances across the dining table all breakfast. I took a breath, glancing down at my coffee cup. The smell was strong, filling my nose. The curls of steam distracting me.

Leo frowned at me, and I tried to smile at him as best as I could. I took a sip and tried to focus on the hot liquid running down my tongue when I saw I couldn't convince him. I tried my best to focus on what everyone was saying, but they're voice faded in and out of my ears. I felt like I was slowly fading through time, because suddenly the topic shifted.

"Are you okay? You look ill," Leo chirped.

"Leo," Rose hissed. "We never say that to a lady."

"Sorry..." he glanced down at the hands in his lap. "But she's so pale," he whispered to her, maybe thinking that meant I could not hear.

"Like a ghost," she widened her eyes at him and smirked. He didn't return it.

I shook my head, eyes still pried open by some other force. "I'm fine, I promise. And I will prove it," my voice quaked and I coughed, "I bet as a ghost I could still beat you at chess later."

He beamed, "you're on!"

The pit in my stomach bubbled aggressively at the coffee I poured into it. I managed to quaff the rest of the cup and excused myself from the table. The sun glittered through cracks in the clouds outside, lighting up half the hallways in Erlot Manor.

And then I stopped walking. The air was thick. Dust was swirling in the light. I felt that familiar icy feeling. I had put on my winter dress as if we were being snowed in, I still felt my teeth chatter in my jaw like loose change in a coin purse.

In the corner of my eye was a face.

I snapped my head to see.

Nothing.

Breathe.

It was nowhere. A faded memory of a nose, mouth, and eyes. All there. Looking at me. Separate from each other but there.

Tears pricked my eyes.

Was I going crazy? My arms shook and I kept them tightly wrapped against my waist, cradling myself like a child.

"What's wrong with me?" I whispered to the air, voice cracking.

The floorboards creaked behind me.

It is just me. It is just me.

I am walking, aren't I?

Then I stopped.

It creaked again.

A gasp burst from my lips, and I moved on, trying to bite back the tears. Give myself enough room to breathe and I could keep it at bay.

It's not there. It's not there. It's not there.

I almost whispered it under my breath out loud, tears blurring my eyes.

I snapped my head round.

Nothing.

Except... was that a frame?

A glimpse of a gilded black frame was hidden around the corner I had just come from.

I frowned. There wasn't a painting there before. The walls of Erlot Manor were mostly bear. In fact, I was positive that there was only one room in the whole of Erlot Manor that held paintings.

I inched closer, step by step, as if it would jump out at me.

There it was. As real as my own self before it.

A painting of a man.

Black hair that curled slightly on top, like it was rebelling against his otherwise resolute stature. He stood, cane in hand, a devilish smirk quirking his lips and boyish features. Young and yet haunted. Eyes that at first glance were worn bright and curious. They reminded me of Leo's; full of questions and wonder. Then I squinted. They squinted with me, their light dying as I watched closely.

I inched backwards. The air felt thicker.

I stumbled back and rang for the maid.

When Anabella finally arrived, she looked disgruntled and hollow.

"You rang, Madam?"

"There's a portrait here."

She frowned, and her eyes seemed to fight the urge to roll. Her neat hands, pressed in her lap together as she stood politely before me, twitched.

"There are no portraits in this house, Miss, I don't know…"

Then her eyes noticed the frame behind me. Her frown only deepened, and she walked forward a few steps and gasped. Her shoes clicked as she all but ran off.

Moments later she was following Rose, who glanced at me, her gaze worried and wide.

She froze before it.

The painting and the statue.

"No," she breathed, her eyes never leaving it. She gasped, and a hand flew to her mouth.

I supposed this was not either of their doing then.

If I had room for rational thought anymore, I would have had to fight the urge to laugh at how dramatic we all were. It was just a portrait. The humour wore off shortly.

"How did it get there?"

There was a pause.

Then she rounded on me.

"Did you do this?" Her eyes were a blaze, wild. "I told you not to go poking around my room, did you think this was funny? Some stupid joke?"

"No, I would never-"

"Because if you did, you will leave immediately."

"Rose, I promise. I would never do this."

My eyes stung at the tears threatening to burst. I felt her heat pulse through me and churn with the cold in my stomach. The bile crept up my throat and I swallowed in back down, taking a deep breath. The room swayed with me, and I held onto a nearby wall.

"Do you think I would really do this?"

When I steadied myself, Rose was whispering with Anabella.

"Go check on him, now. And get Matthew to come take *this* away. I will not have him here!"

She clutched her head, Annabella rushed forward to hold her.

My eyes watched her hands travel to her waist. Those fingers lingered. They were slotted. Familiar. Rose breathed; eyes scrunched up. Her face was paler than chalk and she stumbled forward into Belle's arms.

Anabella glanced at me. Her gaze worried. But what was worried only soon became a smug grin.

I left the room.

Chapter 33

ROSE

14th April 1838

At least the pregnancy keeps George away from me. He gives me my space after hours. That doesn't stop me from locking my door at night or sleeping with my fists clenched under the pillow. When my eyes snap open in the mornings I'm terrified to find myself naked. But no.

I think Belle is aware because she brings me sweet things before bed, cakes, chocolate, hot tea. She sits with me chatting away or playing cards or simply reading together. I really cannot express how thankful I am for that girl. It must be my current position, but I am close to tears at how desperate I am for a friend. I cannot imagine baring these walls, this life all by myself.

In recent times, George has been painting again so I hardly see him. I think I am still unfinished in his studio.

I would think any man would be excited to have a child, but of course, how could I be so stupid? How could I be so calm? All I knew about children was those mysterious trips to hospital the girls would take and how the cries put off many clients. But he kicked.

He kicked.

My baby just kicked.

I braced my hands over my womb and searched for him. Only a layer between us and he felt so close and far at once.

Tears sprang into my eyes, as I felt a balloon swell in my chest.

"He's kicking," I told George.

He glanced up at me across the room.

"Good, that means he's a boy."

Chapter 34

MEG

11th September 1841

The night left me colder. As if a hand was pressing down on my chest, holding me still in bed. I was heavy and hollow at once. My fingers did not feel like my own when I curled them into fists. They illuminated in the moonlight, lying there on my chest. I watched them twitch and move. A shudder repressed itself as a flash of the same hands were on the end of my bed. I closed my eyes and took a deep breath. I opened to peer at the end of my bed. No one there.

No one but me.

Very faintly, though, I heard a muffled cry.

A few choking breaths. A sniff. And then it was very clear to me. A woman crying. Guilt curdled my stomach and I sat up, straining for more sounds. Had I upset Rose earlier? Had the maid told her what I had said about her the other day? Did she wish I'd just go?

The cool wooden floorboards balanced me on top of them, and I strode to my door, hesitant to open it all the way. I peered through the crack, holding my breath captive in my chest. Only when I held the door tightly did I realise I was sweating. I could not feel it. My clammy hands broke away from the door.

I followed the whimpers.

The cool air tingled my skin, numbness glimmering in the wake of the night. As pins and needles cascaded my shins with every step, I floated, my heart hardly beating louder than a whisper to my ribcage. I bit my lip to keep quiet, my chest aching for more air as my heart pummelled against my ribcage. The blood flowed in my veins, but I couldn't feel it pulsate and rush. The shadows scattered every time I placed my foot on the ground. My nightgown licked at my calves, and the anchor in my belly told me I was alive.

The pit opened to scream to turn back. But then I turned the corner and suddenly I was in the entrance hall.

That wasn't right.

I frowned, peering around me, stumbling backwards, sideways and then deciding to keep following the cries. The cries were steady sobs in the distance. Further away. When I went towards the stairs, I turned into the dining room. Wrong again.

Through to the drawing room. The crying was distant but more pained now. I felt a rush shoot through me, and I ran to the corridor, only I was at the top of the stairs now. Hurrying my steps now.

My breathing puffed out, heavy and laboured, I stared wildly at the walls. Dark and looming. They seemed taller. Were they always this tall? Always watching from above. The house shook as I ran again, this time backwards, down the corridor, past everyone's bedrooms and up another set of steps. The newly furbished staircase, that seemed to smell of smoke and acrylic paint as I ran.

The cries were nearer. I was getting closer. Where was she?

I turned to find myself, again, in the drawing room. The window huge and looming. It took up an entire wall. The dark trees shook their heads at me, and I threw my hands down in frustration. The moon glowered and I felt rooted to the spot. A shadow walked past the moon.

I gasped, turning and walking back towards the cries. A sob aching to creep out of my chest, I held onto walls, slid fingers past banisters and skidded across floorboards.

Then I am surrounded by darkness.

It is black. So black I cannot see passed my nose. The air swallows me, muggy and thick, pressed against my lips like the kisses of my childhood. I breathe in sweat and is that my breathing or someone else?

Then I feel a hand in mine.

I screamed.

Light flooding my and screeching in my veins as I flinched and shook.

A light loomed in my face.

Lamp light.

A hand.

The gardener. Mathew's face was there. Peering over me.

It's only then I feel the cold squelch of dirt, soft and wet, in the cracks of my hands. The air slicing my face like a knife, and the trees whisper above me as I lie like a wounded deer on the forest floor.

"How...?"

I gasped for air, the ice stinging my lungs with every inhale.

"It's okay, Miss," he mutters softly.

My blood turns to ice. Blood pounds in my head, my chest mirrors the motions and I crawl backwards, eyes wide.

"No, no, get away from me!"

Are those his hands on me or shadows? I closed my eyes.

"Go away! Go away!"

I screamed and he stumbled backward, face paling in the lamplight. He loomed distantly, eyes never leaving mine, just as wide, like a skull floating in the night. His body a dark tall shadow.

But it was too late.

I whimpered.

I felt the hands on me.

Pulling me to the ground. No. Pushed. Held down. Clammy and callous and rough all at once. Small and slender. Huge and wrinkled.

My skin is disappeared into theirs, melting from my bones. Limbs bound to theirs.

"Get off," I choke back a sob, biting my tongue until blood bursts into my mouth.

I can't breathe. My body forgot.

I lay there, the world spinning from me and into me at once.

I feel the full weight on my chest and his hands slid around my neck. I couldn't move my head away. A dark figure above me, skin disgustingly soft on my cheek, he breathes on my lips. I'm choking from the brandy on his breath. I learnt it's his drink when it happens again.

I'm thirteen.

"It's me, I would never hurt you," I hear him say. Somewhere above me, far away. It's frightened. He's scared.

It's not him.

"Breathe... Please try to breathe."

I try to listen, but my mind is forced to hear the groans and grunts of someone else. I whimper and turn my head sharply away, pushing myself further into the dirt. The mud suffocated my back and hands like a second skin. I shake and shudder as I try not to cry too loudly. They yell when you're distracting them. It takes longer too.

"Miss... Megan? I'm sorry I scared you, I wouldn't hurt you, not a hair, you have my word... please breathe."

There's a hand on mine. I flinch. Flinging myself forward, the icy air hits my back, coated in rain and mud. My mind sears with the touch, as if my skin could scream. But then I feel his hand. I shudder and turn to see him.

Eyes frightened.

I focus on him.

It's Matthew.

The gardener.

I replace the eyes slowly with the frightened and concerned ones above me. In the warm glow of the map, he's looming over my face, I count the lines of grey that are sewn into his iris. I watch the way they drift over my face, taking sharp turns around my lips, cheeks, hair, eyebrows and eyes. There is no intention in them. Only concern.

I took a deep breath, letting my eyes close. His hands stay on mine, but it tightens when I hold it back.

"That's it, Megan, breathe."

I shook. Tears fell down my face. I almost jump when I realise. I looked down at myself and I felt blood rush to my cheeks at the realisation that Matthew was not only seeing me in just my nightgown but also caked in dirt, mud, grass, leaves had fixed themselves to my hair like a crown... I was a mess.

"You gave me the fright of my life," he breathed, shaking his head in bewilderment.

I choked on a laugh and looked at him finally. He was crouched next to me, wary to get closer in case I panicked again.

"*I* frightened *you*?"

He smiled. Then frowned.

"Are you okay?"

His eyes searched my face.

I took a deep breath through my nose, dirt and grass filing my lungs, and nodded, "yeah... I think so."

There was quiet. The world of Erlot Manor crashed down on us both in a second. The cawing of a crow brought me to the outside.

"How did I get out here?"

He frowned before asking, "do you sleepwalk?"

"No," I snorted. I felt pathetic, sitting on the forest floor. I shivered.

"Are you cold? Here," he shrugged off his coat and before I could protest, he placed it carefully around my shoulders. The warmth finally hit me, coaxing out the numb, thawing my skin.

"Thank you," I muttered. Feeling small.

"I found you out here screaming your head off, so I didn't get to see you... walk outside."

I nodded, staring at my hands. My skin itched with the ghosts of hands still on me. I shook them from my mind. I pierced a nail into my palm and breathed again.

"I was trying to find Rose... she was crying and I-"

I looked up at the house to see a face. Only briefly. Grey and white peering at us. Like a mask left in the window. It moved away and it was gone. Again, I could not breathe,

"Did you-"tears filled my eyes again and I dared not blink them away.

This night would not let me rest.

Matthew turned to see what I was talking about. He seemed quiet.

"This house is centuries old..." He swallowed, turning back to face me. "I've heard it said that you can't stay sane in a sane house, and you can't stay insane at the asylum. I think Emily used to say it."

I nodded, "so I'm insane for seeing things here?"

"No."

"Then what?-"

"I said you can't stay insane at the asylum."

"What else did this Emily say?"

He shrugged. "Once she told me," his eyes glazed over for a second. In a heartbeat, he was back. But I did not miss it. "She would say that if you were frightened of the dark you would always be blind. Real wise lady."

"She sounds off with the fairies to me. What was she on about?"

He glanced at me, "I think she was warning me."

I nodded.

"I'm scared but I think I can see... maybe I see that Erlot has a lot of bones buried here."

He regarded me then.

"More than you know, Miss."

I frowned.

"Was I too on the nose?"

We were still crouched on the floor. I did not want to go back inside Erlot Manor.

"She never talks about the ghosts," Matthew whispered. I watched him with wide eyes. His whispers sounded like the trees. Their rustling leaves were growing increasingly loud with every minute that passed us by. As if warning us to go back inside. As if there was a time limit to how safe we were in one place.

"Who never talks about the ghosts?"

"Rose."

"Matthew, I think we need to move."

"Are you willing to go back inside?"

"We can't stay here."

He shrugged, standing up and holding his hand out for me. My fingers ghost over the palm before finally gripping it, and I stumbling onto my own two feet. I felt as numb as a marble statue. My legs rushed blood and I felt dizzy at the sensation.

"Hey," Matthew yelped as I grabbed his arm, stumbling forward. He wrapped an arm round my waist, my skin on fire, but I ignored it.

We hobbled back to Erlot Manor, frozen to the bone, ice in our veins, but equally scared as the other. As much as we knew the other was there, the ice reminded us we were alone.

Chapter 35

ROSE

29th May 1838

We discussed baby names at dinner tonight. And the previous night.

That is how it started again.

I have a few in mind. I like George as a name, it is strong, but I really can't bear the thought of a likeness. Perhaps the name will be the only similarity? And if I do not, then life will only repay me by giving me a replica. Will I give birth to baby boy or will a monster crawl out of me and wait?

They both want to name him George Junior, but I refuse. They cannot hurt me in my condition. I know that and they know that. Which is why I looked them both in the eye and posed many different names.

"How about James? John?"

"Admirable, strong men, a fine name for a boy I'm sure, but don't you think that as his father I get to decide some things?" George looked at me from across the table. Fire in his eyes. But I narrowed mine.

"What about as his mother?"

I turned to *his* mother then. She simply continued with her dinner.

"Wouldn't you think it best that the mother gets to decide these things? I've already allowed you to decide for his career, his education, anything else, but I have to at least have some say, at least just his name."

She smiled. It felt uncanny and strange peeling against her face. But there was a flash of youth to her skin then. A hint at what she was.

"As a *mother*, I can't help but agree, I raised you, George, do you think I could have done a better job if I were a man?"

He seemed lost for a moment. Looking between us both. The pairing you would least expect. Not exactly the golden team you would bet money on.

"No, you did your job."

"I was thinking of other names too. Robert, Mathew?"

The Baroness stopped. She almost flinched. I did not quite catch it as my eyes were dwindling on my husband who was slowly loosening his grip on my child.

She tightened and excused herself.

He sighed, "would you like another cup of tea, dear?"

That night, I got ready for bed, brushed my hair out, and, as I usually liked to do, admired my bump in the mirror. It was then I felt that curdle in my stomach, except dread flashed across my skin, beading into my forehead, my son was with me now.

I looked closely at the mirror.

The sun was dead. The moon hiding in the trees.

Then I saw my bed sheets move. Behind me. In the mirror.

I twisted round.

The room felt so much bigger. So far away. The world was not moving with me.

The doorknob turned.

I stood and watched. Waited.

Footsteps, slow and deep, thudded back to Emily's room.

Thud.

Thud.

Thud.

Slow. And not my mind playing tricks.

Breath left my lungs at once. I fell to my knees, and tears splashed onto my cheeks, my hand clamped over my mouth to keep quiet.

It would never end.

Chapter 36

MEG

11th September 1841

"I feel safer out here," Matthew whispered, as we locked eyes with the stone archway and dark, glistening cherry-wood front door. It was the first time I realised the slender statues of naked women that waited outside the door, watching who entered and who rarely left. Their marble had chipped and withered away with rain and wind; their pretty faces worn to a blank slate that stared vacantly outward.

"I don't feel safe anywhere."

We stepped up the steps. Each step slow and stiff.

"We have nowhere else to go," I whispered, the closer we got to the house the quiet we got. The moon bounced of the statues, causing them to shake with every shiver in my eyes.

The cold snaked its way back inside me and Mathew's hand was numb in mine. It could have been a branch for all I knew then.

"We'll be okay, really, nothing has happened so far to us..." Matthew kept his eyes on the door. I kept mine on the handle. "The first step to being brave is being scared."

"You are full of wisdom tonight."

We stood before the door and, as if to make it more painless, Matthew lunged forward and swung the door open. Heart in my mouth, I watched it creak open. The gaping hole of Erlot's mouth ready to scream at us if we moved a toe out of line. My feet were like blocks of sand, keeping me rooted to the spot. I could not move for fear of something moving. I could hear breathing in my ear. I told myself it was Mathew.

He nudged my waist gently and we walked inside. The familiar coolness was slick on our skin. It was funny to think but walking inside Erlot Manor felt like you were leaving anywhere else. Now it made sense.

My clammy feet squeaked against the polished floorboards. I trod the dirt into the rug and then we creaked into the drawing room. The moon hanging ahead of us, watching us. As if it had followed us and kept a close eye on where we were in the house. I let go of Matthew and sat down in the armchair closest the window, my back was to the wall, and I could watch the entire room and door from here. The shadows tricked my mind through the window, though, and a sudden lurch would grip me as something moved in the corner of my eye.

Matthew stoked the dying embers in the grate of the fireplace, wringing his hands and glancing nervously at me. Finally, he perched on the sofa in the middle of the room. His face pale but nervous. He looked up at me again.

"What were you doing out there?"

I broke the silence.

He jumped. A hand stroked the back of his neck as he avoided my gaze.

"Oh, I heard a noise and went to check it out. My room is on this floor, closest to my work."

I nodded, "what noise? Was it anything...?"

"I think it was a cat, I don't know."

"Oh," I frowned. "You got up for a *cat*?"

"Does it matter?"

He shot me a look.

We were in the silence again, the room filling with questions we did not know where to begin asking. My mind overflowed with the words and what came out was a jumbled mess that made Erlot Manor flinch as I disturbed its quiet.

"Do you ever see or hear anything that isn't actually... here?"

I saw his lips twitch, and his eyes glazed over like before. He took a deep breath, a small smile ghosting his face before he faced me fully for the first time since we'd come back inside.

"No, I see and hear what is actually here. These strange..." he stopped, "why? What have you seen?"

"You first."

"You asked."

"Fine," I sighed, "um," I played with my fingers, "there were these... these hands on my bed," I felt the air struggle to stay in my chest as the memory wormed its way to the forefront of my mind. "I have seen and heard so many things since I arrived... Tonight I heard Rose- someone was crying! Some woman was crying in this house, so I followed it and I couldn't get to her. She got further away. Every single step I took led me the opposite direction I can't explain it." I shook my head. Since when was I crying? "And then I was in the dark, I don't know where I was, I know I was still here, and then something grabbed me, and I was in the garden with you!" I looked at him sharply. He nodded, face sombre and blank.

"I don't want to scare you... again." I winced at the memory. "But none of that was in your head."

"What do you mean? What is this place?"

My heart thudded in my chest, and the armchair felt colder than before. I shuddered and peered around us, suddenly aware of how dark the night was. In London, I was never this alone. I was not alone like this.

"I should tell you that-"

"Tell her what?"

Anabella stood in the doorway. Face pale, hair mussed, but with a stern and stale air about her that made me feel silly for even thinking of the possibility of ghosts. I felt like a frightened little girl again. I felt like a little girl that had had a nightmare and needed to be convinced it was all a dream. I had even needed taking to a different room.

"I was just comforting our guest here. Sorry if we woke you. The poor girl had a bit of a nightmare, didn't we?" Matthew stood up and smiled at me before shrugging to Belle.

I took a shaky breath and tenderly stood on my own feet, suddenly very aware of being in my nightgown. "Yes, Matthew here was just trying to comfort me."

"Well, if you are quite finished..."

I followed her out of the room. Matthew gave me one last look, a hint of an apology in his eyes before slinking off to his own room. Belle led me briskly up the stairs to the corridor.

I really looked at her then. She was so much younger than I realised. Perhaps just a little younger than myself. She was small and fragile, like a doll. Her hair was a mousy brown and her eyes were round. If they didn't regard me with venom staining the iris, I might have thought she was quite beautiful.

"Goodnight, Miss," she nodded, before leaving in the opposite direction. I stood outside my door, and I could not move. My body shook. Tears pricked my eyes. They would be puffy in the morning from crying. My nose was sore and red, I knew that and I was still covered in dirt, though now dry.

I turned around and opened Rose's door. She slept soundly in her bed, her back to me. I crept under the sheets and slid my arm over her waist.

I still could not sleep. I still felt no warmth.

Chapter 37

ROSE

5th June 1838

It keeps happening.

Last time I wrote in here, I described the night it started again. I managed to sleep that night, telling myself over and over it was a trick of my mind. It was the moonlight; it was dark; it was my pregnancy. Anything.

The heat dripped onto my face, the light blinding red that morning after. I lay there, fully

enjoying the ache in my bones. The morning came and I was safe again.

Or so I thought.

I moved my hands from my stomach and stretched them by my side, soft cotton tingling my skin.

I stopped. A hand was still on my stomach.

My eyes snapped open. I looked down. But there was nothing. The feeling had gone as soon I peered over my bump.

I shook it from my mind, and waddled to my dresser, looking through the mirror. Deep dark eyes looked back. Hollow and tired. Veins scarred the white and lines carved tales of the months gone by.

It had been nothing.

And then the night came again.

I blew out the candle and the dark engulfed the room so thick I could not see my own hands. I dared not open my eyes. A part of me still felt silly. Sleep crept slowly toward me, taunting me as my heart quivered with every whistle or creak from Erlot.

I felt watched. But again, nothing happened.

But then the next morning, I awoke to a creak in my floorboards. Another. Then another.

I spoke before I opened my eyes.

"Belle, good morning, you're early." I yawned, turning over.

The footsteps walked to the door.

I opened my eyes.

No one.

Belle did not come for me that morning for another hour.

This has gone on for weeks.

I had to endure card nights and lunches with my husband more and more. He barely looked up at my eyes. The baby would know his voice soon enough. The days drifted past, but I didn't mind. The sun shone down on us for once. The garden had been fixed and Erlot seemed a lot more bearable with golden rays sprinkled through the windows and slipping past the lilies.

But really, when I am finally alone, I feel everything and nothing at once. I miss Meg. I wrote to her the other day, but I try to say as little as I can. She does the same. But they speak volumes to what she must go through all day every day. She tries to keep that part out of it, but I know. The ink is almost seductive against my fingers and last night I dreamt that instead of her letters it was her skin I held close to mine every night. To hold her and feel her lips against mine...

The sickness keeps taking away the time to worry about anything, though. I am so pale and worn away. I thought I was meant to look glowing and youthful, as the doctor told me. But I feel so exhausted, so nauseous every day. From the moment my eyes snap open.

I rushed into the house one night, while everyone was outside. The sun was going down, casting an orange and pink glow across their faces, illuminating their eyes and teeth.

I clutched my hand over my mouth and dashed to the nearest sink.

The kitchen.

As I retched and clawed the wooden sides, the burn of bile stung my lips and coated my teeth, burning my throat. I leaned back, a gasp in my chest, the bitter tang on my tongue. I wiped the sweat from forehead and felt the cool air hit my now damp hair.

Then I saw it. A shadow next to me.

I turned.

The shadow was still there. A silhouette staining the floor. But no one else here but me.

The room stood still.

The light grew scarce. The sun left me. The dark flooded the room.

The pans clattered in the corner.

My heart was in my mouth with the vomit. I shivered as beads of sweat dripped from my forehead and the air stung my lungs.

The room felt thick. Like a blanket, surrounding me. And surrounding me. I was woven into the bricks of Erlot.

The shadow sending my mind spinning. I needed to go outside. To go with the others. I needed air. I needed the servants to light more candles. I needed to get out.

Then it happened.

Just as I left the room.

A hand held mine.

Wet. Cold. Slimy.

A hand let its fingers slide into mine. My teeth clench. A scream died in my throat.

Heart hammering, I fled the room. The air ran from me. The outside was disappearing. Where was the door?

"Help?" my voice croaked.

Erlot became irritated. I felt the change.

The room got colder. The breath stung my throat. The bile rose again. I fell to my knees and retched into the flower beds.

The soil held my hands as I coated the flowers in vomit.

"Sick again?" George was standing over me.

I gasped. Tears blurred my vision. Saliva dribbled from my lips.

I must have looked pathetic.

Every night the darkness came. A silhouette at the end of my bed. A hand on my baby. Footsteps.

It happened every single night.

And now the due date draws closer. Lurking round the corner, smiling at me.

And I dread it.

Chapter 38

MEG

12th September 1841

The day faded into a bland grey that seemed to amuse the house of Erlot. Today, as I peered at his figure strolling across to the bushes, the ghosts seemed to leave Matthew alone for now. I knew I was not alone and yet I felt crazy for ever entertaining the notion. Erlot Manor was the way I remembered it that morning. Did it always change at night? Or was I confused and dazed?

The thoughts were loud and pounding around in my head for almost the entire day, the book in my hand long neglected. I turned pages but my eyes were glazed over and my mind fuzzy. Never had ghosts been real. Never had I been haunted by the dead.

There was Leo in the middle of the room, Annabella watching over him, creasing her dress with that crisp sound that snapped me from my thoughts as she knelt beside him.

"Do you want to tell me what happened?"

I kept my eyes on my book, but they did not move from one word:

help

"But I *saw* her," he doesn't even glance at Annabella. Only keeps his focus on the toy train currently in his hands. Battered and bruised from play, the wood chipping away and worn, paint fading from red to pink. Funny how the signs of love look so haggard.

"What do you mean?" How subtle she is. I tried not to snort. Even turned a page in my book to look the part. Her eyes are so expressive. She didn't wear her heart on her sleeve, it was in her eyes. I was wary of them on me.

I turned another page. Too fast?

"Doesn't matter," Leo mumbled, his fist on his mouth, as his shoulders sagged.

"How about I let you draw? Just this once? I won't tell her," Annabella whispers, a smile in her voice as she bends down to brush his hair. It strikes me how motherly she is towards him. As if he were hers.

He shrugs his shoulders, but his mouth can't fight the smile that's excitedly hiding behind his fist. Poor boy.

As soon as she left the room, I turned my head towards him. He chewed his thumb as he nonchalantly twirled the wooden train, almost grinding it into the rug.

"Leo," I whisper, "what was all that about?"

He looks sheepishly up at me, biting his lip to replace his thumb, which he wiped on his shorts.

"I can't say, it's a secret."

"I'm very good at keeping secrets," I smile, leaning forward. "I promise never to tell a soul."

"Cross your heart?"

I grin, "and hope to die," I say, my face becoming serious as I place a hand over my heart in earnest. His eyes shine at me like black beetles.

He took a moment to ponder if I was worthy before standing and coming to sit on my lap. He leans against my ear, cupping his mouth with his hand.

"Mother is sleepwalking again."

I look at him curiously, his face is deadly serious. The poor boy looks worried.

"I promise I'm not lying; I wouldn't lie."

"I believe you," I smile. "When did she start sleepwalking?"

"She's done it forever," he sighs dramatically. "But it stops sometimes. She keeps coming into my room at night and it wakes me up."

"What does she do that wakes you up?"

"She sits at the end of my bed," he shrugs, "sometimes she stares at me, sometimes she doesn't. It's dark."

I nod, that familiar icy feeling creeping out of my stomach again like ivy, crawling up the walls of my body. "Does she speak to you?"

He shook his head, "no, she never says anything."

"Why?"

"'Cos, she feels so cold."

"Leo," Annabella appears in the door. She raises an eyebrow playfully at him, eye flickering up at mine with a hollow expression. I blanch and nudge Leo to stand up off my lap and go to Annabella.

"Leo was just telling me a story."

She smiled. Only her mouth, though.

"Well, you can draw in secret now, my love," she places the pencils and paper on a nearby table. Leo excitedly hops up into his seat and gets to work. She smooths his black hair out of his eyes, eyes sparkling, her shoulders bent down to him. Then they look back at me and I wince at the coldness that overtakes both her and my veins.

Chapter 39

ROSE

27th June 1838

He's due any day now. Every day I wake up and think "today is the day," but it never is.

Every day I seem to vomit at least three times. Strange how used to that you can get. Tears and sweat streaming down my face. Belle is always there for me with a glass of water.

A few weeks ago, I couldn't bare it but now I just wipe my mouth and get up.

The light dwindled, a light blue cascade of starlight in the air. The cards in our hands enticing smirks from both of us. I won; I don't care if she thinks I was cheating. I was not. Of course not.

As she rose to leave me. The door standing before us, daunting me.

I looked from my hands to her doe eyes.

"Please, stay with me."

She blinked, a smile bright on her face. "Sorry?"

"Please stay with me tonight. I can't stand it."

I didn't know what more to say.

Chapter 40

MEG

15th September 1841

Her soft hand lay in mine, cold as ice, I raised it to my lips and kissed each fingertip.

"You're hard to keep warm," I smirk against her hand. She smiles, leaning her forehead against mine.

"It's not too harsh a task, is it?"

"No, I'd say it's worth my while."

I close my eyes, sighing contentedly as we just lay in each other's arms on her bed. I feel the lace of her cheeks on my skin, scratching me.

I reached up to touch it but she moves away, stiffening.

"I'm sorry, I didn't mean to..."

"No, it's fine, it's just... strange to feel it there."

I nod, eyes looking down at our entwined hands.

"Does it still hurt?"

"No."

"I like the lace," I smile, glancing up at her, biting my lip. She watched me, and I couldn't read her expression.

"Thank you," she sighed. "At first it was to go into town with... I had to secure the finances in person with the lawyer in town... and then I kept wearing it for Leo's sake..."

I nodded, squeezing her hand. She didn't return it.

"He cried when he saw me without it once. I forgot. It was early morning. He used to have these nightmares... they were so vivid; he would say I was trying to grab him and hold him and take him away. Or that this man's eyes were looming over him at the end of his bed. Always the same dreams... I'll never forget."

I winced, the pit in my stomach groaning.

"Poor thing."

"So, he was practically screaming, and it was so early. I- when you're a mother, there's the urgency to get to your child. I could go through the whole of Erlot when it was burning to get to him. It's a strange feeling. And I calm him down, holding him. He then opens his eyes and looks up at me and I feel... naked. His eyes just... they're so innocent and beautiful and it was the first time he saw anything so... so horrid."

I frowned.

"So, I tried to calm him down, but he cried harder. He didn't believe I was his mother..." Her voice cracked and she was silent, inhaling a deep breath.

"Hey," I breathed, leaning closer, my lips grazing the lace. "I'm sure it isn't as ... horrid as you think."

She smiled and patted me hand.

"I'm being serious... do you remember years back, when we were kids... we were new at the Whites'?"

She looked away and nodded.

"And you had been crying all night, you were worried you looked all puffy and splotchy. Which you did," I breathed out a laugh and she smiled. "But you still looked beautiful. You could be... rotting away and I would still think you were the loveliest creation on this earth."

I stopped talking, my face burning. She turned her eyes on me, shining and that smile lifted her entire face. She kissed me.

"George would say that... or similar, in the beginning."

I froze. What else?

"But you mean it."

There was silence for a little while. Neither one of us knowing what to say next or how to say it.

"Meg, what I..."

"Yes?" My breath hitched. I was an inch from her face, blush balancing delicately across her cheeks and nose.

"I try to forget about those years, but I would hate to think that would mean forgetting you."

I tilt my head, "I'm here now, aren't I?"

My gut twisted.

Her hand tightened in mine, her kiss deepened, and my head was spinning.

Years and minutes melted away as my lips kissed every inch of her soft cold skin.

I flopped down beside her, chest heaving, sweat glistening on my forehead, curling into my scalp. I smiled at her breathlessly and she opened her eyes, turning to face me. I mirrored her. A warmth coating my insides protectively. I was still floating. Her half-lidded eyes looked at my lips, smiling as we took each other in. I pulled the covers around us.

"That makes a nice change," she chuckled, pulling the blanket up to her shoulder and nuzzling further into the cushions.

I raised my eyebrow, my nose inches from hers.

"I mean," she looks down, her long dark eyelashes fluttering her cheeks. A rosy glow coats her face, and she is luminescent. As if starlight lives in her, flowing beside me and I drink it in. "I never realised what it could be like, until you came back. And more private here than the Whites' ever was."

I smiled. "Not even your husband...?"

She shook her head, breathing a silent "no."

There was a pause, I closed my eyes, feeling sleep tug at my eyelids. I found her hand and gently prodded my fingers against hers, too lazy to cling on. The bed dipped and the sheets rearranged themselves as Rose shuffled onto her back.

"He's dead now, and he always was really."

My eyes fluttered open. I watched her. She stared at the ceiling. Her hand still resting next to mine.

"When I lay in this bed with my husband... it feels like the other day and forever ago at once." Her brow knit together, "actually, I feel like it's still happening."

"What?" I rubbed my thumb over her knuckles, looking up at her.

"Nothing," she smiled, "don't worry about it."

I leaned over her; words caught in my throat. I wanted to tell her she could tell me anything. I was not afraid of the ugly. I could only guess what he did that made her eyes glaze over like that. I hoped these thoughts were openly expressive in my eyes. But they seemed blank and expressionless to me. They lost their sparkly and the unearthly glow that glistened along her skin had died away. I leaned down and captured her lips in a kiss, hoping she would find those answers there instead.

I awoke in her arms, the blankets holding us together like our own cocoon. Her skin was cool on mine and I shivered when her hair tickled my cheek.

I look up and froze.

"Leo?" my eyes widened. He stood next to the bed, hair messed from sleep and tear tracks shining on his cheeks. Pain slapped him across the face.

I swallowed, holding the sheets to my chest as I sat up, shaking Rose awoke with my other hand.

Chapter 41

ROSE

10th July 1838

Leopold Blackwood is born.

I feel as if I have put everything to the side until now. I have tried my best to ignore the gnawing in my gut. The feeling that I am about to be eaten by a pack of wolves, shrinking myself smaller into the snow, while their teeth shine in the moonlight, begging somehow, they will go.

But they never do.

I feel endless possibilities and dread become kindred spirits in my chest, and every time I look at his face, so peaceful and trusting, I feel stronger. Stronger than I was when Erlot introduced itself.

Chapter 42

MEG

15th September 1841

"Leo... what are you doing up?" Rose gasps as she clutches her nightgown on the floor, her eyes never leaving his, wide and pleading. Should he understand? Should he misunderstand?

"I followed you here," he mumbled, his eyes still on us. I watched in horror. What was he thinking? He was only four years old, but what would any child think of seeing their mother naked in bed with another woman.

"What do you mean, darling? Did you have another nightmare?" Rose's voice strained. Her face paler than the moon. She leaned forward to get out of bed, carefully to keep her modesty, while maintaining eye contact as if Leo were a snake about to strike at any moment.

I watched, my chest rising and falling, my eyes daring not close, heat striking my skin, hand sweating against the sheets that I clutched tightly. The smell of lavender, bed sheets and sweat mingled in made my stomach churn sickly. The only sound I could hear was that of the springs creaking under me as Rose shuffled to the wooden floor, throwing her nightgown over her head.

But then he ran, the soft pads of his feet splashing against the floorboards as he took off out of the room, down the corridor, down the stairs. I stared back at Rose who immediately took off after him, her nightgown falling to cover her completely.

"Leo," she called out, her breath already laboured before she began.

I took a moment to register what was happening and grabbed my own nightgown, flinging the cool cotton garment over my head and searching the corridors for them again, the bitter air whistling in the cracks as I ran past, blowing gently on the sweat that decorated my hairline and hands.

I hugged my middle, walking down the corridor. It looked unfamiliar... my room was not down the hall.

I turned. Rose's room was not either.

Erlot Manor changed for me the second time. The illusions flirted with my eyes, my mind spinning.

"Leo!" I called, my voice echoing back at me off the stone walls, mocking me.

"LEO," I cried out, the breath leaving me completely. Ice wrapped tightly against my throat like a viper. I choked out and looked all around me, holding myself like a scared little girl.

I walked forwards, hoping to hear something. It was deadly silent. That booming, deafening, eery silence. It crawled into my ears like a spider and wove a web in my mind of disgusting possibility. Silence was sisters with possibility.

The dark drew me forward, seductive eyes on me, I clung to myself tighter. I smelt mothballs and dust in the air, the stench growing stronger the closer I drew to the hard-black door before me. Then the clocking of heels on tiles sounded in my ears, bouncing across the walls before landing in my ears. A light illuminated the shadows, scattering behind me for cover. I blinked stupidly as it dangled in front of my face, the black door grimacing at company, and Annabella's face came into view. Large, frightened eyes looking over my face, beads of sweat clustered in my hairlines, tired, dopey eyes looking back at her, lips red and raw from kissing Rose.

I felt naked and I felt I smelled of Rose and what we had been doing. Shame and guilt crawled up my spine and Possibility revealed herself. I looked down at her candle.

"If you were looking for Leo, we found him," she said gently, taking my arm. I was stunned by her softness. I was fully expecting the cold shoulder yet again and here she was steering my down the corridor. She walked me back to Leo's room, where he sat on the bed next to Rose, silent tears running down his face.

Rose had her arm around him, trying to soothe him with soft mutters in his ear, her dark eyes haunting him.

"He's gone now, it's okay," she whispered softly against his cheek, tears spilling onto her skin.

"I saw him, and I saw you!"

"Darling, I was in bed this entire time," she held his hand, but he just stared down at the floor, unresponsive. She had hit a wall.

"*What* did you see, my love?"

He shook his head, more tears spilling onto his cheeks, big black eyes looking up over at me. The power and energy they threw at me, I felt them loom on my skin. I could only look back in earnest.

"I looked out my window, I heard the dogs again-"

"There are no dogs-"

"There *are*!"

He stopped crying, his face reddening fiercely.

"Okay, I believe you, *okay*?" Rose's voice cracked, "I promise I believe you, my baby, I do. What did you see?"

"I saw him. I saw father in the forest!"

There was a quiet pause. Rose stared in disbelief, pain shooting through her eyes, she pressed her lips together and closed her eyes, exhaustion taking her in its clutched. "We've talked about this..."

"I don't care! He was right there!" He jumped out of her arms and flung a pointer to his window, pointing at the trees, dark clusters shivering at the attention. "I saw him!"

"I believe you saw someone," Rose sighed, "but darling, it wasn't your father…"

"Why not? Who then?"

"Leo, he passed away when you were a baby… you know that." Rose's eyes pled with his, and her voice was soft against his ears. But he only stared her down. Tears splashing against his burnt red cheeks.

"I can check if you like."

All eyes looked at me. Rose looked away first. Annabella raised an eyebrow. Leo took a second before his eyes shone my way.

"Please?"

"Sure," I smiled. I took in a deep breath. I took a few steps to the door. "Anyone want to join me, or are you too busy wetting yourselves?"

Belle closed her eyes. Rose smiled briefly. Leo seemed to stop crying for a second.

I walked up to the window, looking past our ghostly faces gaunt and drained in the candlelight licking at our features.

Then I watched him walk out of the trees.

He came towards the house.

I stood about to leave, watching from the drawing room window. Rose held Leo against her chest, rocking gently as he sat in her arms. Annabella remained the torch bearer. Not that the candle was a match for the moonlight.

I gasped as the moon caught his face.

"It's Matthew," I whispered excitedly. "You saw Matthew," I looked over at Leo whose ears pricked up.

He silently walked to the window, and he seemed relieved and deflated. His little shoulders rose and shrugged as he realised.

"You see, darling," Rose cooed, her eyes pleading for him to come back to sofa to her. "It was Matthew all along."

"But" Leo bit his lip, "what about you?"

Rose frowned, silently walking to him.

"I saw you... and your face wasn't..."

Rose looked down, her fingers twitching, blush burning the edges of the lace sewn into her cheek.

"I know, but that was just a dream..."

"No, it wasn't! Stop lying!" Leo's face was aflame with indignation. A small ball of fury. "When will you stop lying?!"

He ran to Annabella, who froze like a deer trapped in the headlights.

She froze as the little boy took her hand and tugged. He wanted her to put him to bed.

My eyes napped back to Rose.

I watched as shock became confusion became disgust.

Daggers aimed right at Annabella.

"Put him to bed."

Annabella hesitated.

"Goodnight, darling, I will see you in the morning, when you know how to talk to your mother."

Rose waited for Annabella to turn away. Leo was frowning, his little face scrunched up and red, staring his mother head on.

Finally, Annabella turned and floated from the room, Leo dragging her away.

"Sometimes I worry I see an all too familiar face in him," Rose muttered, not looking at me. She stared at the doorway. "Do you think we are born bad?"

"I don't know," it felt suicide to cut the stillness of the room, so I stood like a statue as Rose cooled off. Erlot Manor seemed to wait on her command. Everyone held their breath, including the shadows.

"As for Matthew... I should explain, it's what he does. It's why he stays here overnight."

I frowned but did not dare speak.

"He lost a lot in this house. It was before my time."

"Oh, I'm sorry for him, I had no idea, but why does he stay then?"

"We don't talk about it," there was an edge to her voice I did not like. My insides recoiled and I felt the ghosts of bruises rise on my skin as her voice mirrored tones of the past.

"I understand."

Matthew walked past the room, and I rushed to him. Rose floating up behind me.

"Why were you out there? Leo was scared, he keeps seeing you there," I started. Hardly knowing what I really wanted to know. Is it the same grave I saw the other day?

"I'm sorry for disturbing you ladies," tilted his head, a genuine grief passing across his face. He then stepped around me, trying to quickly leave.

"Why do you go at night?"

He paused and turned his head to glance over his shoulder at me. Rose was silent, regarding him with a look of austerity. She held a chin high and raised an eyebrow. She looked porcelain. Like a marble statue.

"I couldn't sleep," he said after a while. I let him go.

Chapter 43

ROSE

12th December 1838

It was then I thought about the letters, the paintings, the death certificate and the pills. Not to mention Belle's own memories. I wasn't safe here, but where could I go? I had no one, no money; nothing. The weakness flowed in my veins, and I felt my mind screaming at it to stop; this feeling of help-lessness took over me like the sedatives did. I popped one into my mouth, the sugar sweet on my tongue as it slid down my throat. I lay back and tried to force all poison from my mind. I didn't want to be another Emily, I also did not want the same fate, but I couldn't leave. If I had lived in blissful ignorance...

Leo was asleep, ignorant of the world, in his crib next to my bed, the moonlight casting a glowing cage of protection. Only to be abruptly woken a few hours later by his cries. Each night, I nursed him back to sleep and heard the footsteps again. I held him to me well after he fell asleep. Every night since he was born.

The months passed with him in my arms, the Baroness hovering like a crow in a cornfield. George eager to take me to bed, I would lay there and endure the pain, it still felt tender down there. But he didn't care.

Each night I felt Emily's presence, yet I never felt more unnerved than when he was in the room.

The Baroness went away early for the evening. George, Leo and I stayed while the fire died out and crackled. He was apparently reading (but drinking seemed to take more focus).

Leo refused to be quiet or still.

Wiggling in my arms when I held him, rocking him gently. I tried to get him to feed, but he only cried harder, and shook his head away. His mouth opening to reveal a cavernous hole where nothing but wailing and screaming came from that night. I held his face over my shoulder, cradling his head, trying to burp him.

It was so violent in my ears. All the while, dread slid up my legs and arms like an icy snake in the room.

George was staring at me. His face grey, drained, alcohol very nearly spilling from the glass from where his hand limply held it over the armrest, his eyes dull and bloodshot as they moved between me and the baby.

I kept Leo in my arms. Tears pricked my eyes.

"Shhh, it's okay, mummy's here," I whispered, bouncing him lightly, trying to look away from George. He stared. Unblinking. And sighed.

"Maid, take the baby, would you?"

I looked up at Mary, who stepped forward to take my baby. Her eyes were strange. Pleading? Or pity?

"No, I can calm him. I can." I shook.

"Take him," George sighed.

Mary stepped forward, "It's okay, I can lay him down to sleep, if you like, Miss, he might be tired?"

She smiled at me.

I only looked at her, my eyes blurring with tears. Why did I feel so helpless?

"I'll go too, he needs his mother."

Another sigh from the corner of the room.

"And not his father I suppose?"

I swallowed and exited the room.

I saw his fist tighten round the glass, as he rolled his eyes and took another swig. I could almost taste the burn from here.

It took hour still, well into the night, before Leo calmed. I started to cry with him, both of us shaking together.

And then the night came.

When he finally fell asleep, cradled by moonlight and blankets to guard against Erlot's insurmountable icy draughts and permeable cold that only August seemed to cure, I passed out in my clothes.

My stomach churned and the shadows that crawled over me the moment the candle blew out whispered venom into my ears.

The door clicked shut.

I kept my eyes closed enough, peering to see white.

White hands, white shirt and trousers.

A few strides and he was on top of me. I lay still, begging for the screams to still in my throat. I waited.

I prayed he didn't hear the whimper that stifled itself against my lips. My eyelids heavy from earlier, but I tried to keep still, his hand already pinning my wrists to the bed, a sharp jolt shooting up my arm.

Leo did not stir.

He stroked my hair, leaning to kiss my cheek and throat. Every touch of his lips made my insides squirm, my blood stilled, my heart forgetting I was alive for just a second.

The smell of brandy entered my nostrils, and his smooth, clammy hands descended to under my nightgown.

I could not disguise my breathing when I realised what he was doing, when he lay on top of me again, his cheek sliding onto mine, I blinked and whimpered.

"George?"

It was his move. I was rooted to the bed.

"Shh, it's okay," he mumbled against my neck, the soft whisper sending a wince writhe through me. He parted my legs with his hand and moved to enter me.

That's when I bit him.

Hard.

"Stupid bitch!" He cursed through clenched teeth, hand flying to his shoulder.

I ran as fast as I could, stumbling from the room. My footsteps slamming against hard wood. Copper filled my mouth, brandy still stung my nostrils, my throat was dry as a bone, as I felt my mind push me from the room.

Tears pricked my eyes, as I grabbed the key before leaving, swiftly turning it and slamming the door quickly behind me.

Emily's room.

I locked it and held my breath.

I heard him leave my room, footsteps slowly nearing me.

A tear escaped my eye, and I gasped as it splashed the floor below me. He paused outside the door. The light underneath blocked out by him.

I backed away. My bare feet sticking to the wooden floor as I peeled them off with every step back from the door. The Winter air filled my lungs, ice cooling my hot skin and twisting my stomach, slicing my veins.

I shook my head. This was not happening. This was all a nightmare. He would leave me alone.

The doorknob shook, "Rose?"

My eyes didn't dare to blink. The night air froze every tear that ran down my cheek, salty on my tongue. I stared in horror as eh rattled it again and chuckled.

"Darling, it's okay to be nervous. Open the door."

I bit down on my lip until copper leapt onto my tongue.

"I promise not to touch you again, just open the door. This is silly."

My back hit wood. I looked down to see the snow glittering back at me in the dark. The crows in the trees nestled but watching me. I let out a cry as I tried to calm my breathing.

Where would I go? What would I say?

By anyone's mind, my husband was claiming his rights.

One look at the door and I saw a shadow pass through it. I turned back to see the outdoors. I could jump. End it now. What was I really doing by hiding?

"Rose, let me in!"

"Rose," the wind whispered in my ear and I climbed over the window ledge, gripping the wood till my knuckles burned white. I edged along until I found the wooden lattice of dead roses and clung on for dear life. I looked down and felt my insides freeze. After a few steps or more, my hands and feet stung from thorns, blood dripping on the snow as I slipped.

I groaned.

I landed on my thigh and squeezed my eyes shut, biting down on my lip as I squeezed through the pain. A shot of lightning and the urge to vomit soured through my stomach. The snow held me in its cold embrace, breaking my fall. I winced, turning over to prod at my thigh. The bruise moaning against my skin and crying until it would be purple the next day. My teeth chattered as the air washed over my wet night-gown, clinging to my pale skin like a new-born.

I crawled out of the grave I'd made for myself and stood shakily on my own bloody feet, stumbling into the night, holding myself. Where would I go?

Tears froze my face, my cheeks painfully twisting and red, the blood dropped from my hands and spread itself wide as a stain on the soft snow. It oozed from my toes and I shuddered. I would die here if I stayed.

A crow cawed above me.

I could not run to the police without evidence of anything. I was underwater, drowning, and no one could even see me. Let alone save me.

I dragged my feet through snow, growing more numb to the world by the second, my hair frozen to my forehead, eyes painfully frozen, as I stared back at Erlot Manor. I banged on the door and pushed my way in when someone finally answered. I fell to the floor in a pathetic heap, gasping as I clutched my leg. The heat of fire in my veins upon seeing the Baroness coming towards me was enough to warm me up as I sat there, hunched over in a pile like old laundry.

"Get her a blanket," she demanded to the butler at the door. He nodded and skulked off.

I glared at her, wishing I was able to stand and face her.

She watched me with cold steel, piercing into mine, but I was already bleeding.

"Mrs. Blackwood, what were you doing outside at this time? It's much too dangerous and cold for young women such as you."

Before I could answer, George was by my side. His hair quickly smoothed back; a repulsive grin plastered across his gaunt face.

"Afraid that was my fault, mother," he held out his hand for me and I begrudgingly took it. My skin green at the feel of him yet again.

"Gave the poor girl a fright."

"Do be careful George." She smiled at him, her cold gaze returning to mine. "Your wife is awfully jumpy."

Chapter 44

MEG

15th September 1841

Before he could fully disappear, there was a loud bang of the front door. I jumped, whipping round on my heels. The front door.

We all stopped. The door had always been closed, surely? I would have felt the cold...

I opened my mouth to comment when a tap at the window echoed from the drawing room.

I turned again to see. No one there.

"It was probably just the trees or something, dear," Rose huffed a nervous laugh, staring at me.

Then another thud. Upstairs.

"Still trees?" Matthew raised an eyebrow, turning to Rose. Her eyelashes flickered, her face paling as she stared at the ceiling.

Another thud.

Thud. Thud. Thud.

I gasped and bit my lip as it got closer. Was something coming down the stairs? It sounded like a boulder bouncing on the floor above us.

I turned to Rose, who only maintained her widened eyes on the ceiling. It did not shake.

Mathew glanced at me for a second.

"What is that?" I breathed, trying to breathe slowly. I felt the air shift in the room. We were so exposed in the entrance hall. The polished marble, the cold stonework, the windows...

"It's gone now," Rose breathed, but her eyes still did not blink.

Thud. Thud.

"Sure."

We all waited, drifting closer to one another like clouds in a storm. Minutes passed before we felt safe enough to turn our gaze away from the stairs.

"It may have actually stopped now," Matthew muttered under his breath.

"I don't feel safe enough to go up there..." I whispered, biting my nail.

"Don't blame you," Matthew sighed. "But, we can't stay here all night."

I shook my head. None of us moved. We stayed like that for a few more minutes. It felt like years.

Then a scream pierced the walls.

"Leo," Rose breathed before rushing up the steps.

My legs followed, rushing me up the stairs for her, Matthew by my side.

Rose banged on the door, shouting for her son.

"Let me in!" Rose screamed, rattling the doorknob and wrapping her knuckles against the door. The door shook with all her attempts and Leo's sobs could be heard between knocks. Frightened and broken on the inside.

Matthew reacted immediately, springing to Rose's side and pushing on the door.

Then, suddenly, the door swung open, Matthew and Rose clumsily stumbling inside.

I peered in.

The dark was like a mask.

Slowly my eyes made out the grey shadowed form of Leo, crouched by the window, cowering with his knees pulled under his chin. His body shuddered and he tightened his grip around his knees with every wrack a sob threw through his chest. His lily-white fingers curling into his knees, denting half-moon bruises there.

"Leo," Rose breathed his name the way only a mother can. A sharp mixture of grief, concern, anxiety, worry, affection, and a softness that only comes from a "you're alright" or an "I'm here" that I have never figured out. She tugged his body to hers, but he only cried harder, tears glistening in the moonlight like snail trails on skin. He stared at her and shook his head, distraught.

I watched in horror as he cowered away from his mother. Rose only frowned and dipped closer, shrinking to see his face.

"Darling, it's me? I'm here now, it's okay."

He shook his head, squeezing his eyes shut as more tears spilled onto his face. He flung his arms to the ground, snapping his palms against the wood and flew from the room, running into Annabella's arms, who stood stunned behind us.

My eyes widened, turning back to Rose.

"What is it? What is happening?" Annabella's shrill voice made Rose flinch, who stared at her son. Her eyes glazing over, the brow knitting together. Her lips quirked down.

"There was a noise," she swallowed. "I came to see if Leo was alright..."

"Oh, dear, what is the matter?" Annabella cooed, bending down to see Leo's face. He only buried his face into her stomach and clung onto her tighter.

"It's okay, shhh," she brushed his hair out of his face, and I watched Rose as it stabbed her. She swallowed the pain and smiled.

"Leo, what is it, darling? It's me, your *mother*," she tried again, her voice shaking.

He turned, poking an eye out to look at Rose kneeling on the ground a few paces in front of him. It was like watching a lion tamer. "It's me, mother, I promise to make it all better, what happened?"

Her voice was completely different. The warmth laced with a whisper reminded me of smoke when it washed away into the clouds. Delicate. But the strain in her voice broke through and shattered the image.

"Mother?" He choked out, a small whine from the crying cracked his voice. He had stopped crying, but he still shook like the way Rose's voice did.

"Yes, darling," she smiled, brightening.

He unclasped his hands from Annabella, who stood still. Her eyes watching keenly.

Leo took a tentative step towards his mother. His little fingers rose to touch her cheek. They caressed the black lace that hid her burn. His face was blank. A few deep breaths struggled their way from him, though.

Rose shuddered at the touch. But remained still. Her hands twitched.

"I'm sorry," he whispered, hanging his head, his hand falling by his side.

"Oh darling," rose flung her arms around him, pulling him tightly to her. She stroked his black hair out of his face and kissed his cheeks. "What happened?"

"You were there... but it wasn't you... you locked me in and you started coughing..."

I frowned, looking up at Matthew who seemed blank and unresponsive. He just looked over at Annabella. Her eyes were far too absorbed by the touching scene to notice us.

"I think it's best that you stay with me tonight," Rose said, looking up at us. Leo held her hand as stood up. "Everything will be okay, but Leo needs to be with me tonight," she sniffed. Annabella nodded.

Chapter 45

ROSE

12th December 1837

I shuddered in his arms, as he insisted on carrying me to my room. My breaths hissed in my throat, and I hoped I was too heavy or too unbearable cold or I made his pyjamas wet. I needed to see him in discomfort. I wanted to thrash in his arms and push him away and run free again. I wanted to show him the letters I found and have him confess.

I wanted to be Rose Mallory again not Mrs Blackwood.

I change my mind. I didn't want it anymore.

I glared at him. My pitiful, red-burst cheeks, lips, ears and nose, frozen hair and eyelashes, alongside my shivering limbs did nothing to help my venomous gaze. I was like a scared lamb to him. Only guiding his painting further, like she had slipped out of the canvas and fell into his arms, clinging to him for dear life. I would have scratched him, gripped his shoulders until they bruised blue, but my fingers had shrivelled into my palms. All I could do was glare.

I frowned. This was not the way to my bedroom. I turned, wide eyed, the Baroness was still with us, the pathway was getting darker, but her candle flicked the shadows away from our path. Faces of Blackwood's gone by flickered over me on the walls and I shuddered. Veins set alight with a new lease of life I writhed and struggled against my husband's arms, but he only held me tighter, and a strangled yelp escaped my lips. His nails dug into my flesh and my bones ached where he was crushing me. I looked back at his mother, she was looking ahead, not one hair out of place, her dress perfectly presentable and her wrinkled skin pulled back tightly, thin lips in a hard line. I could not faze her.

"Mrs Blackwood, when young girls do irrational things as you tend to do… sneaking around at night, disobeying your husband, disobeying me by extension, and trying to run out in the dead of night in the freezing cold…" She looked me in the eye, "they need to be kept an eye on."

My voice stuck in my throat I could only widen my eyes as I looked to see her swing open the door of the basement, steps descending downward into black nothingness.

"Now, you understand, the Blackwood name can never be tarnished. I've worked hard to keep this family respected. In time, you will also understand."

George slowly carried me down into the abyss. I felt screams struggling to crawl up my throat. Further into Tartarus I was forced, the light of the Baroness illuminating above me; forward seemed only blacker by contrast. The feeling in my fingers sprang back enough for me to push hard against George's chest and arms, scratching him, pounding my balled-up fists against his chest, striking his collar bone. He flinched and gripped me tighter, his nails digging into my skin.

"Stop, let me go!" I finally choked out. "You can't do this!"

"Oh, we can," The Baroness breathed, disinterested in my struggle. "You need to learn to behave, Mrs Blackwood. Women who show as much irrationality as you do not birth good children. We need to fix you before it's too late. Can't have the village thinking that about you or us, can we?"

I gritted my teeth and glared at her. "You think I'm crazy?"

She smiled. A sickly, toothy smile. Her face was too tight, too fixed for this and yet that sickly smile hung in my mind, even now writing this it lights up the forefront of my mind, the flame licking each tooth, so it stood out in my mind, even when I was alone in the darkness.

"Who wouldn't?"

The air left my lungs at that; they could and would prove me crazy to everyone if I made a case against them. The devious poison that ran through Blackwood veins was infecting me. Was I being irrational or was it all true? I curled up tighter to myself. George placed me down on the cold, hard concrete floor. The loss of human contact caused an empty pit to desperately open inside me as the shadows crawled towards me like rats.

As the door began to close, the basement swallowed me up.

"Wait," I called out, my voice like a frightened animal, "leave the candle at least."

The Baroness paused. I saw a look waft over her face like a mist. It was only there for a second. But I did not miss it.

She walked to me slowly and placed it at the bottom of the steps, holding onto her sons arm as they both left me alone. The click of the door behind them echoed all around me and I shivered as nothing surrounded me. The darkness scattered where the candle hit and I huddled over it, eyes wide, not daring to blink.

"Calm," I whispered to myself it burst into the black abyss as a whimper.

I took a deep breath. And then another. Inhale, exhale, inhale, exhale. Focus.

I looked around. A vast nothingness stood before me, mysterious and enticing; seductive but deadly. I could not tell if the shadows scattered miles away or ended just next to me. I steady my hand as I held the candle, slowly gathering myself up off the floor.

My nightgown was still damp, clinging to me, I fiddled with it trying to get it to stop sticking to my skin. I bit my lip as I brushed the fabric down. My wet skin felt like ice as my thighs brushed together, red, and raw with every movement. My shoulders moaned against my skin where I'd been crushed against my husband. My hair tangled behind me, falling over my eyes in an icy heap. Blood and skin under my fingernails, the taste of copper and his slimy skin still was bitter in my mouth. Hands and feet like blocks of ice against the scrape of concrete below me.

I took a few steps forward, looming the candle in front of me in an outstretched arm. A rat squeaked and scuttled past me, echoing as it went. I turned, looking for it. Gone. The basement was playing tricks on me.

I took more steps. The soft padding of my feet echoed, and I had to shake the horrible feeling of someone behind me. My stomach clenched with the feeling looming over me.

Waving the candle suddenly I kept looking around as I slowly made myself about. I did not dare stick my other arm out. What would the Blackwood's keep in a basement? I shuddered to think.

The tap tap tapping of water echoed ahead. Dripping down and splashing the ground. I crept towards it and the soft glow of my candle illuminated a face.

I jumped. A gasp left my body and I moved forward again. The candle illuminated the face but as I squinted in the darkness, I realised it was not a human face. Or at least it had been made to seem human. It was a small mechanical person, sat on a ledge. A friendly smile carved into the metal, cogs for ears and round child-like, hollow eyes.

My mind was ablaze with memories, filtering in so many times that I could not distinguish the memory from the dreams from the nightmares. My eyes flicked over the mechanical toy until the word automaton sprang to mind and I eyed it warily. My stomach convulsed as my mind raced. I leaned in to see its hollow eyes. Nothing.

I prodded its stomach and it moved.

I gasped.

The slowly churning of wheels and cogs filled my ears in the silence as the little automaton stood up. It's metal arms, stomach and legs shaking against their cold joints.

It slowly lifted his hands. And clapped. One. Two. Three.

And then I realised.

This was the same automaton my father liked to make for me.

Jumping back, tears sprang to my eyes as I was met with vague memories blurring together in my mind of him.

His straggly white beard static on his face, as he smiled, a wry dry sort of smile, eyes dark and hollow into mine. He would bring me one and show me it, clapping and I'd giddily clap back.

My mother would watch us. Always.

Then I remember waking in the middle of the night to her taking it away from my room.

She would tell me to not accept anything he was giving me.

I never understood. And now I'm not sure I want to.

I bit my lip as I remembered the painful stab of my mother, I would have liked to know her, but Fate really did have it in for me. And now I was trapped in a basement in the middle of no-where with one of his machines. It watched me and a sinking feeling filled me to the brim. I could not stand it here. I could not stand it anywhere. Tears rand down my face, their salt slipping into my mouth and the blue stretching the automaton wider before me.

I bit my lip, frightened to hear my own sobs echo back at me mockingly, blood burst down my chin and I wiped it away with icy hands.

So, she had suffered the way I did now?

She burned with him and that was the harshest trap of them all.

I shook my head, sobs wracking my body, as my knees collapsed below me. I had trapped myself in Erlot Manor, where my mind was being scattered along dark corridors, crashed into broken mirrors and moulded by paint.

I gritted my teeth. My portrait. The portrait. I was some weak doe he could hunt.

Then, I thought, my tears stopping, *let him think that.*

Slow breath in and out ceased my shaking ribs, and I gasped out, face looking up at what should have been the sky but there was nothing but black, and I felt the cool stale air on my wet cheeks. I wiped them away hurriedly and tried to rake my fingers through my hair. I didn't know how long I'd been down here, but it felt like hours.

I waved the candle over more automatons, each springing to life more fragments of my father I could lace together. All these gifts he would bring me. Who was he?

I trod the path along the wall of automatons, each with black eyes following my every move. The candle flickered against each face, moving their expressions from empty to happy to angry to sad. I blinked when I found a curious human sized one, slumped in the corner, cobwebs weaved through its eyes and mouth, dust disguising it as part of the grey wall.

I loomed over it.

Its jaw creaked.

I yelped.

A spider crawled out of its mouth and down to its stomach, scuttling away into the shadows. I shivered, wincing at the sight of its huge mass of blackness wandering off. I turned away and back to the automaton. Something was inscribed on its neck. I leaned forward, narrowing my gaze under the jaw. The words 'For Wilhelimina' were carved into the automatons metal, rusting over. Frowning, I looked further along for more of the message, but it had rusted over.

The automaton groaned and I leapt back.

The jaw fell open. As if it too were gobsmacked.

My candle flickered over the insides, and I saw a piece of parchment poking out of its throat. Narrowing my eyes, and with nimble fingers I slowly pushed my hand inside its mouth, wincing and biting my lip as cobwebs tickled my wrist and dug under finger nails, sticking to my skin.

I pulled my arm away to reveal letters.

All in a small stack, tied with brown string neatly.

I smiled; this could be something more. This could be something to damn them all.

They were addressed to Wilhelimina Blackwood and... Wilhelimina Mallory. My mouth hung open like the automaton next to me.

I tore the letters from their string prison and hungrily read them.

Placing my candle on the floor, I sat and carefully read the words.

Dear Wilhelimina,

I am away again on business, and I have devised that if you cannot give me a son, then I must find other means necessary to produce an heir. Yes, our daughter is lovely, and she grows up fast. Not fast enough for me I am afraid. I will find a new wife. As part of my condolence, I wish not to be seen as the cruel father of the family for abandoning my daughter. I have made allowances for you to stay in Erlot Manor and given you enough money to ensure you cannot hate me for the rest of your life. However, on the account that I am successful in producing a male heir, the Manor and the money will be returned to him as is right, and I am sure he will decide to give you something if he wishes.

Yours sincerely,

Montague

I frowned. This was a very formal way to abandon a wife and daughter. Unattached. Guitless.

I ran my finger across the ink. The pitiful words of so-called care in leaving her his house but with the horrible reminder he or his son could take it whenever he felt like it. I shook my head as I grabbed the next letter.

Dear Wilhelimina,

I see you have changed the family name to your own maiden name. This is disgusting and abhorrent to me. First you wound me by not giving me a son, and now you strip all memory of me from the family I gave you. I have found myself a new younger wife, more fertile and she is already pregnant. It should surely be a boy.

Do reconsider changing your name, I am sure my son will not be happy to learn of this news when he is of age.

Yours sincerely,

Montague.

The annoyance penetrated every line.

Dear Wilhelimina,

It has been many years and it is only now I hear you birthed me a son! To not tell me is to defy God and his way if this is what he chose for us.

He is my only heir. My wife could only birth me a daughter and it has been many years of unsuccessful births and pregnancies later that I write to inform you I must see him! IT is urgent.

To deny me this would be the cruellest crime. To the family name. Which you seem to have forgotten all about.

Yours sincerely,

Montague

I trembled. The Baroness and my father?

Vomit climbed up my throat and I choked to keep it from bursting from my lips, shaking my head as I felt myself pale and slide to green. I froze, knees numbing and wobbling on the spot as ghostly hands traced over the letters.

My husband was my half-brother.

Chapter 46

MEG

15th September 1841

We all hovered, hoping she wouldn't banish us.

Matthew stood near the door, slumped over. Annabella stood near Rose and Leo, waiting on their every whim when they needed. Her eyes looking over to me smugly now and then. She had her place here; I had no use. I stood, hoping to stay. How could I face being alone? How could I hope to sleep after everything that had happened tonight?

"She'll come back," Leo whispered, as rose tucked him into the bed. The side I had been sleeping in over an hour earlier.

"She can't," Rose clipped, smoothing the sheets over his chest, smiling down at him. "Not while I'm around. And if she does, what will she do?"

Leo gulped, almost cartoon-like, looking smaller and smaller the more he stayed in that bed. The sheets seemed to swallow him, and he was wading in a sea of cotton.

Then it began.

A loud banging. Against the door. Frantic, ferocious, and feral. I gasped, stepping away from the door. Matthew jumped, all eyes on the door. My heart flew to my throat. I hoped the door was locked, my eyes frantically darting to catch Matthews', who's hand went to the doorknob, clicking the lock in slowly. The noise stopped.

Then the doorknob rattled. Leo whimpered, Rose clutching him to her chest, trying to shush him as she too stared wide eyed at the door. Annabella drifted to her side.

It stopped.

I stared at that doorknob as if it would fly off the door at any moment. I tried to see if any light could betray whoever was behind the door underneath. But it was pitch black all around us. Black except for Annabella's candle.

Tap. Tap. Tap.

It was at the window. The curtains did not flinch.

Then it was the walls.

Banging. Thudding. Scrabbling on the floor outside the door like a crazed wild cat desperate to get to us. Desperate to devour us. Feed off us.

I choked on air. Eyes glazed over; the darkness made my head spin. When would it all stop?

The scrabbling and scraping coated my ears, and crawled inside my throat, bile rose, and my head swayed with all the direction the echoes of desperation came from.

"Leave us alone!" I yelled. I waited with bated breath. The whole room waited with me.

The noise stopped.

Then one, dull thud sounded behind the hidden door.

Rose's portrait room.

I breathed deeply, turning to Rose, who's eyes flickered from the door to mine. Dark, shining eyes. Never had she seemed so terrified. Her doll-like demeanour slipping to reveal flesh and bone. The black lace mask looked so stiff on her then.

"Matthew," I turned back to the door. He stepped closer to me, silent. "Do you think we should...?"

He breathed, slowly, drawn out. Had he been holding it that long? He did not say a word. Did not move. We simply stared at the door. Both of us knowing we *should* look. What else was there to do? Part of me was still thinking there had to be something... rats? The wind? That lie felt better than the impossible truth.

I stepped forward, taking a deep breath, my lungs catching all the air and locking it tightly in my chest, as every nerve n my body sprung eyes to watch me. The hair stood on my arm as I reached up tentatively. My fingers hesitated as the cold metal hit my fingerprints, dust placing me at the scene.

"Don't," Rose gasped. I turned to see her, teary-eyed, hand clasped over her lips. Her eyes pleaded but remained on the door. Then she nodded.

I nodded back, turning my attention back to the door. I could feel energy buzzing between my body and the other side of the door. The shadows in the room lurked, excitedly scattered around my skin. And I froze.

"I'm right by your side," Matthew breathed, it was quiet enough for me to hear and loud enough for me to turn the doorknob and swing the door open.

My eyes adjusted to the darkness. Anabella remained with Rose. Then the grey shapes appeared.

Squares of all shapes and sizes sat in heaps. The canvases.

Faces stared back at me. Their eyes watchful and reproachful. Adjusting the light that entered on them. Their shapes hit my eyes and in a flash I stumbled backwards.

"Rose, did you turn them over?" I tried to breathe in and out. In. Out.

"No..." She was still with Leo, who was quietly sobbing into his mother's chest.

Matthew walked closer. His eyes caught something.

"Is that?" He mumbled. I followed his gaze and squinted at a portrait.

"Rose," my eyes widened. "What is trying to grab your attention?"

There was a portrait that stood the proudest. In front of a heap in the middle. The clearest face in a mirage of eyes. Watchful. Her countenance younger but faded. Her eyes watched ours and moved with me.

But it was the background that made my heart skip a beat.

Fire.

Chapter 47

ROSE

12th December 1838

The light crept in faster than the slow creak that echoed into my ear. It slid. Making palms enflamed in sweat, as I waited diligently at the bottom of the stairs. Head held high, dress flattened out and hair combed out. Obviously, my nightgown was dirtied and still damp from last night, creases blessing my figure by hiding my curves from the leer of the male servants and my dreaded husband. My hair perched on top of my head clumsily, each curl fighting another curl, each strand strangling another strand until a bird's nest was formed. My eyes were sore from crying and my mouth felt acidic from vomiting. My throat scratched itself desperately, and I had to swallow a million times to be able to form a sentence when the Baroness stood before me, eyeing me up and down. The letters were tucked under my arm inside my nightgown, lacing my clammy skin there with papercuts.

"Good morning, Ms. Blackwood," I smiled, hoping light could still find its way into my eyes once again. My hands were clasped neatly in front of me, which both let me shield myself and cling the papers to my side.

"Good morning…" She raised an eyebrow. "There seems to be excellent improvement in your disposition, Mrs Blackwood."

"Oh yes, I have learnt my lesson and I see now I was being awfully stupid. Why I was perfectly irrational, wasn't I?" My throat threatening to close with every sound.

She smiled back at me, "well, that's good news." There was silence between us, steely eyes flickering over every part of me, daring me to move of flinch under such a stifling gaze. My bones groaned against muscles, every part of me ached to lie down on a soft bed, for the sun on my face, and for a glass of water.

I hoped my smile was bright on my face, I felt myself wince the longer she took, my body swaying on numb legs.

With a bath and a brush, I could look the part of a submissive daughter-in-law a lot better; this was the performance of a lifetime. I felt like a prostitute again, playing all the different types of women men dreamed you to be.

"It appears you have improved your disposition."

I followed her carefully up the stairs, where daylight burned, and the same paintings seemed to smile at my tremendous recovery. An applauding from the past for survival of the present.

Teeth gritted behind my lips, I kept my arms glued to my sides, desperate for the paper to keep still. I had the horrible gut feeling that the Baroness had ears like a hawk and one whisper of paper against fabric and I would be found out. I focused on my breathing the whole way down the corridor, where Belle met me with sad eyes, silently leading me back to my room with two other maids. The door was opened for me and the maids and Belle immediately set to work to draught me a bath, light me a fire, and lay out my clothes. Belle left to grab me a glass of water without me needing to ask.

I turned away from the maids and walked to the other side of my bed, by the window, letting the letters slip out from my nightgown where I kicked them under the bed. With one quick glance back the maids to make sure I hadn't been seen, I lifted off my nightgown and sat on my bed, naked. Belle returned and slipped my robe over me and handed me the water which I drank like a thirsty dog, leaking over my chin and dribbling down my neck. The other maids wrinkled their nose.

"Where is Leo?" I gasped, lowering the glass, "where is my son?"

"He is here," Belle rushed forward to take my glass. "I took care of him through the night, don't worry," her eyes looked deep into mine. I knew she meant that she really guarded him. "He's asleep now."

I looked over to the cradle to see a glimpse of a sleeping body, tucked up, legs poking out of blankets.

I smiled; the ache eased just a bit.

Once in my bath, I eyed the maids warily and covered myself. They nodded and left. Leaving my cup of tea, which I gratefully gulped down.

I unfurled and let the water wash over me. Take away the ice, the snow, the bruises, the feeling of vomit and George's chalky skin on my teeth. I closed my eyes and felt like a baby being cradled by its mother after a shock of crying.

When I opened them again, Belle was peering through the keyhole.

I didn't need to ask why anymore. I never would question Belle again.

She walked towards me and knelt, taking a slippery hand in hers.

"What happened to you?" She felt my forehead with the back of her hand. "Do you feel weak? Did they give you anything?"

I shook my head, which felt heavier than a ton of bricks at that exact moment, "what did they tell you?"

"Nothing, just that you had a bout of hysterics and were being looked after for the night."

I rolled my eyes.

"Was that all?"

"I was told to take care of you when you came out."

"Thank you," I whispered, tears springing to my eyes. I blinked them away, looking down, hoping she hadn't noticed. "You must not have slept."

"I wouldn't anyway."

I nodded.

"They trapped me in the basement," my voice was barely a whisper. I had begun to feel surrounded in Erlot Manor. I didn't need evidence of silhouettes and footsteps sounding in the distance to know that I was being watched and listened to.

"Did...." Belle swallowed, "did they at least give you a light?"

"Yes, they're so kind," I bit bitterly. "Belle, I found something very important. Something worse than we thought has happened."

I nodded my head, tears springing to my eyes again. The past night washed over me as I remembered the painting of me, George on top of me and then the basement and the letters. Everything filtered through my mind in non-linear fragments; pieces of a puzzle I never asked for. My mind felt scattered, and I pinched the bridge of my nose, steadying my breaths.

"I found letters from my father to the Baroness, detailing him leaving her and how he never knew about George... George is my brother."

Chapter 48

15th September 1841

"Who set the fire, Rose?"

Silence had passed. Our minds had wondered on different pages, and all come to the same question. I was the only one to voice it.

Rose drew herself up, Leo long abandoned on the bed, shivering, while Annabella swooped in as a surrogate.

"It was an accident," she said, her voice measured and subtle. She had rehearsed this a dozen times or had said it so often it became a catchphrase in her throat. Readily supplied.

"Doesn't mean someone wasn't to blame," Mathew said, sat in the chair by the window, his head in his hands.

I shook my head.

"Did your husband paint flames as your background? Was that really there before?"

Rose lowered her gaze, her hands resting in each other awkwardly.

"Something, I don't know what, is trying to say something... to *you*, Rose."

She lifted her eyes to meet mine and they seemed hollow. No light or shine. An announce of fear shrouded her pale lips and hollow cheeks.

"I can explain," she began, sighing.

"There's *something* to explain now," my mouth hung open. "The past two months I've been here you have shrugged off all of these... strange happenings, and *now* you tell me there's *something to explain*." I throw my hands in the air, really drinking her in. She was a statue.

"Meg, please," she tried to grab my hands, but I shrunk away, regarding her coldly. I narrowed my eyes.

"Don't... say what you have to say, but don't..." I shook my head, walking further away to slump in a chair on the other side of the room to Rose.

"I thought it was me, my mind finally snapping... And you *let* me believe that."

She stood, eyes pitifully shining at her hands, not meeting mine. I felt the cold grasp at my insides painfully twisting my stomach until the bile rose in my throat. I felt the heat rise on my face, my ears burning. A confused twist of temperature mixed inside me.

She remained silent. Her eyes refused to look in mine. Her face flushed.

"Whatever this is," I couldn't help but notice Annabella looking more worried by the second, "I need you to understand that I can't control it."

"What does that mean?"

Matthew frowned at her.

"I wish I could explain... especially to you Meg, but my mind... it's like this house...I know you've tried to walk around at night, I've heard you... I've seen you, it's a maze. Erlot Manor likes to play with your surroundings, manipulate itself, it's seductive but poisonous. It feeds on you until *nothing* is left. I need you to understand that my mind is like a fog since I arrived here... I can't think clearly."

"What does that have to do with-"

"Meg, do you remember when you asked me why I never leave this place?"

"Yes..."

"It's not because I don't want to, it's because it won't let me."

She took a shuddery breath, her lips quivering. Those black holes seemed so broken like cracked glass, but I couldn't look into them. It distorted whatever was held inside or beyond.

Then I realised.

"Every time I go to the door or even if I get as far as the outside gate, I end up somewhere else. If I leave the front door, I'm in the dining room.... You know."

She didn't greet me that first night.

"I sound and feel crazy, so it has always been easier to just pretend this all makes sense. Let myself fade into the fog, become a part of Erlot Manor. It's easier than trying to fight it... But since you came, it's as if the house feels disturbed. It can sense your rationality, this newness about you," Rose stepped forward, crouching and reaching for my hands. I felt numb.

"It is trying to-"

"I think it's best we all calm down and relax," Annabella made us all flinch. Her doeful eyes stiffened, a glassy film protecting her from the smoke we could all smell. "I think we're just a little excited now, what with the strange noises. I read a terrible storm was supposed to be coming our way in this morning's paper," she made her way to Rose's side, roughly forcing her to stand. "I say we all need some rest, look how the sky is already lighting up."

I watched Rose's shoulders slump and her eyes look down at her feet as she shuffled into bed next to Leo, who had cried himself to sleep already.

Matthew did not dare look me in the eyes. I tried to stare at him, will his eyes to mine. Anyone. Surely, I was not the only one who needed to know more?

But one sharp look from Annabella and I clamped my lips together. Another time. I did not know how I could sleep after all this. But I could wait until Rose was alone again.

I hesitated before slowly pushing myself out of my chair, the harsh cotton of the cushioned seat scraping my clammy skin. It felt like the only real part of this situation. I caught Rose's eyes and my heart skipped a beat. My blood flipped a switch.

"Well," I muttered, rushing up to her side. "Can we have a moment to say goodnight?" I don't look over at Annabella. I already know she's bristling. But, she was still a servant. Still had no choice but to leave when Rose dismissed her. Matthew had slipped from the room unnoticed.

"She's waiting outside, she won't give us long," Rose whispered, her eyes darting to the door.

"I believe you," I whispered, and her eyes widened, the light returning slowly and unsurely. She looked down at her feet again. "Really. I have noticed that about the house. I believe you. But I need to know more." The cold lace the breath that passed between us. "We can't live like this."

She nodded, biting back a smile. I leaned forward and pressed a gentle kiss against her cheek. Soft and wet from the tears. I smiled at the delicate pink that tinged her cheeks as I pulled away.

"Here," I smiled at how breathless she seemed from a simple gesture. "Take this," she grabbed something from under mattress, a book. Thrusting it into my hands, she held my gaze, dark and intense. "don't let her see you with this."

I looked down and flicked through to see her handwriting coating every page in black ink. It was her diary.

I slipped it under my nightgown and covered my arms over my waist before leaving. I did not look back. I avoided Annabella's eyes as I walked back to my own room, eager to flick through Rose's own words.

Chapter 49

ROSE

13th December 1837

I left my room later that day, while Belle waited by my door, peering through the keyhole in case someone would come to find me.

I locked Emily's room behind me, my skirt swishing around about my ankles. I stiffly turned to watch about the room. The white light of the snow's reflection glittered about the room, and it was much different to the room that shielded me the previous night.

I checked under the bed. The scratching was gone.

I frowned and turned back to the drawers, hoping to find something else. I roughly glided my hands along the sides, top and back of the drawers hoping for more secrets to tumble out.

Nothing.

I sighed and knelt to feel under the bed. Pausing a moment when the room seemed to spin away from me, I squeezed my eyes shut. My insides lurching at the sensation. I'd been feeling strangely ill on and off since Leo's birth. I took a deep breath and opened my eyes again.

Even started squashing the mattress for something.

Nothing.

I knelt there for a moment longer, trying to think of where Emily would keep something secret. Where any woman would keep something secret, but they were all gone.

That's when, quite when I was going to abandon the idea and head back to my room, my eyes landed on a very strange wooden panel. Under the bed, the skirting board, being so dark I hardly noticed, there was a carved, subtle line. Lying flat on my stomach, I pushed myself under the bed, hair falling into my eyes, forehead perspiring, as I reached my hand towards it.

I tapped it lightly. It was hollow.

With both hands pressed up against it, I dug my nails into the slit and pulled. I thought my nails would be pried from their fingers before it would budge. But with a slight 'pop' it came free, and I smiled in victory as I carefully set it down on the floor and lay my eyes on the dust and cobwebs that decorated the hollow before me. A shudder ran down my arms as the spider in the basement from last night, walked his wiry legs across my mind.

I took a moment to breathe, feeling just how small the space was under the bed, as if the bed was lowering itself on top of me, about to squish me slowly and surely. I bit my lip and dove my hand inside, letting a scared yelp die in my chest. I grabbed something I was sure was a book. My nails digging into the hard leather.

My shoes scraped the wood, as I pushed my body out from under the bed. My dress fighting to stay there. I sat back on my heels and blew a dark strand of hair out of my face as the dust followed closely and wafted inside my nostrils and throat.

I shook myself, as I found it wasn't a just book but a diary.

I could have cried with joy to find it was Emily Blackwood's personal diary. I tucked it safely into my pocket and crawled back under the bed, clumsily pushing the panel back into place. I pressed my ear to the door, listening for any footsteps or breathing on the other side, then peering through the keyhole for confirmation.

I fled the room, locking it and dashing into my own, where Belle jumped back from the door, staring at me with raised eyebrows. I nodded, excitement dripping from my face, as I pulled the dairy out of my pocket and prized it under her nose with two hands.

"Oh," she beamed at me, "have you read it?"

Her hands trailed over the cover as if it were made of glass.

I shook my head.

"Grab the letters," I nodded to my bedside table.

We both excitedly curled up by the fire and read. Belle dove into the letters while I read through the diary. I let my eyes eat hungrily at Emily's words; each punctuating a similar experience to my own over the past year.

Today has been yet another nightmare. There was even a storm lighting up the sky all day, as if jealous of the sunlight. I was with Belle, and I told her to keep the fire going for me, as I was to go fetch her a book, I'd left downstairs, when in comes George almost white hot with rage.

He kept saying how I was being foolish to say something in town. People were talking (they were not). Then he was quiet, his eye looked toward Belle. But then I said "no, don't stop on her account, tell me all about your delusions today."

Then he hit me! Struck me right across the face. Hard. There was a red mark on my face all day and it smarted. It has stopped now and died down, but I had to rouge the other cheek to a tomato to match it up in time for dinner with mother. She even told me I looked like a harlot with all that makeup. I wish I could have told her her perfect son is not so perfect as she thinks.

I wish I could go to town more; my friends are there every day without me now. But I have to help George out with his paintings. How many do I have to sit for now? He's done a million of them. Today he suggested I do a nude one... Part of me is excited (imagine the scandal; I think mother would have a heart attack) but it would just be another part of me he takes and keeps for himself. I dread to think of him keeping it in his room and looking at me whenever he wanted. But, as mother said, I have made my bed. I used to be excited by him, but now he refuses to leave me alone.

I tore my eyes away for a second to picture Emily Blackwood. She was devious, even enjoyed how forbidden and illegal, maybe disgusting her affair was. She seemed the type to thrive on chaos. But there was a part of her I recognised in me. A helpless, trapped part that George could never retrieve. He'd created it after all, and it is best to leave our creations alone.

Belle caught my eye, "he sounds so controlling..." She nodded to the letter in her hand.

"Which one?" I snickered.

A split second of a smile reached her lips before she frowned again.

"Do you think this is proof enough? Of something?"

"No. Not yet." I bit my lip, "I have a horrible feeling they... did more... maybe, poisoned her. And I know you feel that too. We need some sort of proof of that. *Specific* proof."

"I saw it..."

"Believe me." I looked at her, memories of Meg and the orphanage bit my mind hungrily. "Police won't care if any of us say anything. We need a lot more proof."

She was silent a moment. Her doe eyes flickering from the diary to the letters to me again. She didn't quite meet my eye when she asked me, "have you had experience of this before?"

I looked back down, my hands toying with the corner of a page.

"When I was younger, my friend Meg, we were both at the orphanage, we'd just turned thirteen. One night, this woman took Meg away, but she came back to us... She couldn't speak. It was agreed she was allowed to stay there that night before she had to come back, and they used the words "made her bed." I didn't know what was going on, did not fully know until a year later I got to find out for myself and join her."

I felt my forehead flash with sweat, as I focussed on the page.

"She looked no older than twelve."

I paused, looking up at Belle who seemed to have leaned forward, sympathy and curiosity written across her face.

"They pay more for that."

How I hated them.

I flushed, looking down again and continued.

"We shared a room, and I woke up in the night to her crying. Doing her best to muffle it against her pillow, you know. So, I crept out of my bed and wrapped my arms around her, she flinched and cried again so I came round to face her and tried my best to soothe her. When she stopped crying, she finally told me what happened."

"You don't have to tell me if you don't want to." Belle stared at me; I couldn't bear how pathetic I must have seemed. I looked up, staring into the fire. The flames licked the chimney as I clenched my jaw.

"The woman who took her away ran a special kind of brothel in London, ones I now know are everywhere, where men pay extra for a young virgin... She'd been drugged and woke up in the night to an old man on top of her..." My eyes stung, remembering how Meg struggled to tell me anything at all. Her body froze, her throat closed. The words weren't allowed to come out. The truth was already blurring itself and the memory thrashed in her mind as her eyes kept staring through me.

I held her as she silently shook. Eventually, she fell asleep in my arms. The story was practically the same as mine. And too many more after me.

"That's horrible," Belle whispered, "what happened after that?"

"We worked there. George was a client. I got away. She didn't."

Belle looked horrified, her mouth hung open, her eyes glassy as she stared down at her hands in shock.

She leaned forward to press her gentle hands in mine.

"I'm so sorry, Rose."

I don't know how long the silence hung between us.

It would hang itself up inside my brain like one of my husband's portraits. Meg's paint had stained my mind and eyes to the world around. The pink-tinted world of a thirteen-year-old girl had been melted down and made into my wedding ring. I was awakened very early to where evil lurked and found that it too often stayed out in the open. The sins I'd been taught to avoid were merely hobbies to these people. These men. I let the silence hang, hoped it was enough to commemorate and imagine a life for Meg she should have had. Instead, she still must close her eyes and pictured home, whatever that could be. I told myself that whenever I could, I would take her away with me. My helplessness hung itself up in my mind too, across from Meg, staring directly at her. It sickened me.

There was shuffling that entered my ears and woke me from my pitiful daze. I got up and swung open the door to see the back of Matthew's head running quickly away down the corridor. A glimmer of a spy before my eyes. I shook my head, turning to Belle, quickly closing the door.

"I think I know why the gardener is trapped inside Erlot Manor in the Winter again."

Chapter 50

MEG

16th September 1841

My heart clenched at the words.

Rose so painfully tries her best to be honest, but the fear laced the ink in every letter. The way that man took her and ... even when she was sleeping... vomit curdles in my throat, threatening to rise and I cough, stilled on my bed. But I need to go on. I need to know what more happened to her since she left the brothel. Anger coursed my veins as I read all it all. I devoured her thoughts under candlelight, the clock ticking me on, though, my lungs winded by the nightmares Rose experienced.

But I couldn't help but feel Annabella or 'Belle' was so changed... how young she seemed. This was only five years ago... Now she is like a hawk, watching our every move and drifting in the hallways with her candle, always ready to tear me away from knowing too much.

The last words linger in my mind.

This must have been her old diary if it ended before the fire. What happened in the fire? Did Rose set the fire? I shook my head, she wouldn't... Another part of me felt she was justified in doing so.

So... these ghosts were plaguing her still, even when she had submitted herself time and time again. Until she has completely wasted away and nothing of her is left but smoke.

I slide off my bed, feeling as I am floating, book in hand, returning it... the sun shone through my curtains, the true morning breaking in the cobbled walls of Erlot Manor.

Chapter 51

ROSE

13th December 1837

I placed all the letters inside my dress, safely buried in the deep pockets I had been sewing in my moments of boredom. I tugged my little black waistcoat down, the brass button standing proudly up at me. My blue dress swirling around my ankles, I took off down the corridor unsure of my next action except to confront my husband about Matthew. My head felt a little light and dizzy, as I usually did these days. My insides still churning against me every day.

I checked the dining room, the conservatory, the hallway, the drawing room, and knew exactly where he would be. I headed up the steps, my little black boots tapping against the marble of that oozed out from the entrance way like a frost. Sweat began to tingle in my hands as they reached to knock on the door. With one last pause, knowing this would change my life forever, my hand hung in the air like the thought. I then wrapped my knuckles against the door, wood grains stroking my hand, the paleness of my hand clenched in a fist against the mahogany like the moon in the night sky, looking at me expectantly.

Closing my eyes and taking a breath, I entered.

"George?"

He was studying my portrait in depth. Brow burrowed, hair messily piled on top of his head like a nest, apron doing its

best to keep his white shirt from getting paint on (and fail-
ing miserably). His hands were caked in paint, all congealing
together to make brown and black at his fingertips. Brush in
hand as he nibbled the end in thought. I stood there a while,
invisible, as he watched my painted self unblinkingly.

I coughed.

He jumped. Paintbrush flew to the floor where it blobbed
red paint in a messy dollop, and his apron crinkled as he
turned to see me. For a second, he looked angry. But only for
a second.

A smile broke out across his face, and I saw he was tinged
pink from working hard all morning. He smoothed back his
hair but only managed to smear paint across it. It now lay
flat against his head, caked. Once black shiny hair was now a
mirage of colour.

I tried my best not to laugh at him.

With him standing there so earnestly, I hardly knew how to
begin. Part of me felt if I saw this George all the time, I could
say nothing. But I also knew there would be a lot more than
just flashes of anger in my future. And I could not forgive him
for what he did to his sister and possibly being the reason he
she is dead. I looked him in the eye, then decided to glance
down at my hands shyly, eyeing up the portrait.

"How am I coming along?"

"Oh brilliantly," he smirked, then turned back to the portrait, waving his hand around at it, at me, "I've almost finished
you."

I stared at him.

"I came to inform you that I think the gardener, Matthew,
has been spying on me." I watched his face pale, and then
another smile forced its way through his lips.

"Oh, I'm sure he hasn't, what on earth made you think that?"

I bit back a frown, and shrugged my shoulders, "I caught
him looking through my keyhole, and more than once I have

suspected him. I can hear him walking to and from my door now and then."

"Are you sure it wasn't your imagination?" He looked at me keenly. "Those sedatives can leave your body strangely; I've seen it happen. It's probably all in your head. Next you'll be telling em that you've been seeing ghosts."

I bit my lip.

"I *saw* him."

There was a pause. "He might have been walking past your door as you saw him!"

I drew myself up, keeping my head high as I regarded him. He watched me, keeping his smile on his face, his façade of the accommodating husband. I shook my head at him.

"There is another thing I wished to discuss." I took a breath as he waited for me to continue. "I know about you and your sister," I began slowly, carefully selecting my words. Before I could finish, though, he had taken a few paces forward and I paled as I saw that look again. The same one as the night I bit him.

"What are you on about now?!" He cried angrily, very close to my face. I took a few steps back. Always good to keep far away from the teeth of the beast.

"I have read her letters, your letters, and her diary, and I know what you did to her and I know she was pregnant with your child-"

"Shut up!" He leaned forward, regarding me. I held my breath. "No, you haven't."

I smirked, "is it not proof enough in your defensive manner?"

"Will you just *stop* meddling," he spat through gritted teeth like a viper.

His eyes narrowed; his pupils dilated. The cloudy sky outside winced as I edged close to the window. I would soon run out of space to run.

He took a deep breath. I held mine.

"So, what are you going to do?" He clasped his hands together, his face hazing over with too many emotions. I was quite frightened by all the masks I found he wore. "Go to the police? They would never believe you. Your word is as good as your honour, orphan."

It was like a punch to the stomach. All the candles that flickered in the room seemed to be chanting at me. I didn't know if they were on my side or his. That was when it hit me.

In one swift motion, I grabbed a candle and threw it at the easel. As he turned, I took my chance to run, not turning to see how my face melted in the blaze.

"You little bitch!"

I kept running, loud thuds reverberating all over Erlot Manor. I found myself in the entrance hall as I met the Baroness there.

"Where do you think you're running to?" She hardly looked at me as descended the stairs.

"Just on my way to talk to you, Wilhelmina."

She looked up sharply, her features like daggers raised towards me. But a sickly colour entered her cheeks. It appears she wasn't much of an automaton at all. But definitely a hawk, watching her prey.

"Where did you find my name?"

"I read it in your husband's letters." I stared her down, heart hammering against my ribcage and pounding in my ears. "I read them *all*."

She didn't get a chance to react as George appeared, smeared in paint and red in the face, as he grabbed my arm and yanked me to him, paint smearing against my dress as he shook me. I stared in horror at him.

"George, take her away."

"Where?" He spat, still staring down at me.

"The nursery, far away from trouble."

I narrowed my eyes at her, as George threw me over his shoulder and carried me upstairs, the smell of smoke, paint and alcohol filled my nostrils and I gagged.

"I know he was my father, Wilhelmina!"

My dress was stained with yellow, red and blue and black paint. All swirling together in chaos against me.

As he sat me down, he grabbed my chin, smearing even more paint on me, staring me down. I held his gaze, not daring for a second to let him know I was frightened.

He left, locking the door behind him and I was alone with a crib, small windows, and the dark.

Chapter 52

18th September 1841

I knock on the door, and all I hear is a gasp and quiet patters of feet before Rose's face appears in the crack of the door. She watches me nervously, biting her lip when she sees my awe-struck expression and her book in hand.

She then let the door swing open, eyes looking over her shoulder.

"Come to mine," I whisper without hesitation. I glance at Leo, who has never looked so peaceful.

"If he wakes up..."

"I won't keep you long," I smile.

We tip-toe back to my room, where, as soon as the door closes, I wrap my arms around her. She is stunned, I feel her melt, her arms wrapped around my waist, chest to chest. Eager to let it be known we can't be parted.

She leans her head against my shoulder, her dark coils tickling my cheek. We stand there for years, holding one another. I wanted to tell her how sorry I was, how angry I was for all that had happened. That had she written with the truth I would have appeared immediately. I would have whisked her away like a knight in shining armour. But the words echoed in my head and never translated correctly to the tongue. Instead, I kissed her cheek and whispered a thousand apologies, while she squeezed her eyes shut against my neck.

The sun dwindled on our bodies, and she let go, breaking away from me, her eyes looking down at her hands, which had begun to fiddle with the sleeve of her robe now that it wasn't draped on my waist.

"We need to leave this place behind, Rose," I breathe, holding her by the shoulders. "It's not good for you to stay here, not good for Leo either."

"I know," she sighed, she seemed to stiffen, "I have a feeling I can never leave."

"We could try to…"

She frowned, head snapping up.

"You would run away with me?"

"Haven't I already?"

She bit her lips, as I smiled.

"We should at least try," I lowered my voice. The thought seemed to make her more and more unsure. She shrunk away from me, inward on herself, growing smaller and smaller. "Here, go get dressed, and pack your things, we can order the rest to wherever we end up." I made a motion to her to the door, she nodded, a smile pulling out from under her teeth.

Chapter 53

ROSE

13th December 1837

There I was. The next woman to haunt Erlot Manor, her screams stifled by the shadows and her eyes blinded by the ice of its perpetual Winter. I stood there, breath unfurling smoke from my lungs, heaving slowly. I could not process how time had passed me so fast that day. One moment I was with my husband, watching his face slip of many masks and now I was confined to the nursery. I looked at the windows, so small, like they were poking out from the floorboards of the room below. I felt along them for any sort of catch, banging against the glass, hoping it would budge. My mind flitted to Belle, was she aware I'd been stuck up here? Were they suspicious of us?

I struck the glass again, but they were sealed shut to the stone of this place. The cold glass curled around my fingers as I pressed them against it, peering down below. All I could see was white. Snow surrounded me, clawing its way along my body, inch by inch. I shivered and sat back on my heels, ready to give up. The air left my body, and I felt tears prick the back of my eyes yet again. I was so tired of crying, of feeling weak, of being isolated. I swatted the tears away.

All the time in the world was with me now, as I sat there and Fate looked sadly down at me, almost ashamed of me or even herself for what she'd put me through. I turned back to my room and curled up in a ball, eye on the door. I had one chance to confront the Blackwood's (or the Mallory's) and I had failed. Locked myself in my own prison.

I felt dizzy standing too long. So, I sat and stared around. Such a still room.

The crib stood there, eerily waiting for me to peer in. The open top and closed sides only forced more shivers from my person. I shook my head. I was too old to believe in all these ghost stories. I had been stupid and naïve. I had played their game without a proper strategy, and they had taken my king. I sat there a few moments. The sky very quickly transformed itself from grey to lilac to deep purple to sunburnt red and finally black. A plumage of colours in its hand. I was still sat there, biting back tears and feeling sorry for myself. A few more minutes of deep breaths and I shook myself. I was not stupid of naïve to believe that George and his sister were nothing but that. I was not stupid to think that we possibly shared the same father. I was not stupid to think Emily Blackwood had not died from TB. I narrowed my eyes at the thought and knew I had enough to go on. If I did not leave this house, I was going to be another Emily Blackwood. And I had a horrible sinking feeling, like an anchor to my chest, dragging my back to that floor, that I already was her.

I was about to find some sort of object strong enough to smash the window with when I heard footsteps outside the door. I stood there, unsure of what to do if he came back. Surely, he would not subject me to more of his antics in a nursery. In his dead child's nursery?

The doorknob turned, squeaking against the metal and piercing my ears as it filled the silence. I watched as it swung open. Brown hair followed pale small hands, that curled around the frame as she looked into the room one side and then turned to find me, a small smile on her lips when her eyes met mine, relief washed over her shocked face.

"Come quick!" She cried out, her face changing back to a morbidly serious one. I followed her, out footsteps softly pattering as we circled down the stairs like scared doves.

"How did you know where I was?" I gasped as she tugged me down the stairs and we wound down corridor after corridor, my feet stumbling to keep up with her.

Before she could answer, though, George was in our way.

He stumbled across our path, stretching himself across the way, his eyes weary but watchful and I gritted my teeth.

"George, please just let us go." I pressed my hand on Belle's arm.

"You can't just leave," he spat, "you are tied to us now, you are my *reputation*. If you leave, you will ruin me."

I shook my head, "I won't tell a soul, I will change my name, I'll go far away from here. Just let us leave now!" I begged, eyes pleading. Tears in my eyes, what would they do to me this time?

"I suppose you'll take my son too?"

My heart stopped.

"Please, where is he?"

I saw him thin about it but then I also saw his arm flex towards me. Thinking fast, I dodged his arm, taking Belle with me, as we knocked over a candle on the window ledge to our right. Before I could acknowledge the flame falling against the curtain, we had taken off running down the corridor, twisting and turning inside the labyrinth of Erlot Manor, except this one was unclear as to which monster was the Minotaur. I was ever watchful for the Baroness; I had no idea if she was around the next corner of far off on the other side of Erlot Manor. I was wary that George could be behind us. Without footsteps echoing all around me, I did not know if were safe or still in danger and so we kept running until hands hit a stone wall and I collapsed against it. Heaving, we did not dare look anywhere but behind us. He had not followed.

But then it hit me.

I smelt smoke.

My head fogged up. Leo. I needed to leave. Now.

I looked up. Erlot Manor had been created with stone but also wood. Everywhere was a beam or two of mahogany staring back at you. I looked to Belle who seemed to already have caught on and I took her hand, as we cautiously, walked down another corridor, knowing it led somewhere close to the entrance way. When we were met with nothing but darkness, I span round. It was so dark at night, that I could not even see the way we came.

"Where's Leo?!" I almost knocked her over as I grabbed her shoulders, nose to nose, eye bulging. Agony swept through me every moment I didn't know. MY mind trying to flash pictures of a crib engulfed in smoke that I tried to shake.

We were blind to the world and smoke was crawling its way towards us. It was falling from the ceiling like fog creeping towards us in the graveyard. I coughed and spluttered as the room we'd ran into filled up with it.

"I-"

Then a beam fell. Barricading the door with fire. Trapped.

I squinted, sticking my hand out in front of me as we kept on, the firelight giving us some light to go on. I could see a door out of the room, and we pushed against it, landing somewhere else, where the fire had already engulfed. I tightened my grip on Belle's hand and she did the same. She grabbed her napkin and held it against her mouth and nose. I looked down and decided to shirk off my waistcoat to do the same. It was not the best device, but it would work until we found a way to get out.

It was then that Matthew popped up out of the ashes and stood before us, shouting something. The roar of the fire threatened us and stumbled back a few steps. I burst into tears, as a weight lifted. In one of the maids' arms, behind him was a little bundle, wailing against the heat and the roar of the fire, as she desperately rocked him in her arms.

Leo.

"Jump?!" I yelled when I realised what he was saying to us. I shook my head, waving my hand at the fire, looking at him as if he had gone mad. The moment my foot went near the fire it swept up at my skirts, trying to grab my ankle. I pointed behind us and at the windows to signal we had nowhere out.

He disappeared.

"No!" Belle screamed, staring all around us. Her back to my back as we turned slowly, praying for some good idea to spring to mind. I looked across the room to where the fire glinted at the dinner table, creeping across the room closer to it. And then I saw the candlesticks on top. Without warning, I let go of Belle and grabbed them, giving one to her.

With one look back at her, I aimed at the window and smashed it open, she did the same and we were suddenly hit with a cold sweep of air against our faces, fighting with the sweat the fire had doused us in. Except this only meant the fire that framed the window now roared against the air that intruded. I bit my lip, ready to throw something else.

But then Matthew appeared again. Apparently impressed by our initiative. Throwing handfuls of snow against the fire, he did his best to keep at bay enough for us to climb out. I hoped desperately for him to hurry as the fire lit up like a Christmas tree behind us.

I turned to see it creeping towards us, licking the floor-boards at our feet.

"Quick!"

I grabbed Belle's hand and urged her through. She looked up at the fire that still threatened to get at us.

The heat seemed to burn me up, sweat spilling down my back as I fought for air in my lungs, which seemed to shrink in on themselves.

"Go!" I pushed her, Matthew grabbed her torso and lifted her out, stumbling backwards onto the snow together in a heap. With a bite at my ankle, I didn't need a push. I hoisted up my skirts and stepped up onto the ledge.

The fire licked my face like a hungry wolf, and I yelped as I jumped out into the snow, quick to grab a handful of snow and melt it against my cheek, my eyes stinging against the pain. Belle held my other hand, urging me to get up on my feet.

At a safe distance, all we could do was watch as Erlot Manor crumbled to the ground. Wood snapping and collapsing. The Fire crackling and roaring like a lion who'd won the pride over at us. I looked about at the rest of the people of Erlot Manor, except it was just us.

The only survivors of Erlot Manor.

Chapter 54

18th September 1841

I yanked my suitcase out from under the bed, throwing on a dress and making myself a lot more presentable. Which, from the nightmares of the entire night before, was a challenge in and of itself. My eyes were scribbled in red ink, dark circles hugging my eyes, lips faded and as chapped as my palms.

The floorboards creaked under my feet with every movement, the house sighed as the wind blew past every nook and cranny. The cold sunlight dazzles the windows and blinds the dusty shadows that lurked in my room.

In less than an hour I met Rose by the front door, our suitcases at our feet, while Matthew called for a carriage. We had money. We would go anywhere. Try the next town for a week. Plan later, I told her.

Annabella was making all kinds of excuses.

"What about Leo? He needs to be in his family home, surely?"

Rose shook her head, her eyes alight with stars as they remained hook on me.

"We could stay in town or further away for a little while we look for something more permanent."

Annabella did not need to utter a word when the sarcastic expression told me everything I needed to know about her view on the matter: you already have somewhere more permanent.

The carriage arrived and Matthew loaded our bags onto the back. My mind ran a mile a minute with how we needed to leave. Leo looked tearfully up at the house. His face taking in the windows. My mind tried to stare up at them with him, but a shiver ran up my spine at what the little boy really saw. Was he frightened? Was he worried about leaving? Did he want to stay?

Annabella stood, rigid, at the door. Her eyes shining at Rose and Leo. But she seemed worried... her eyes narrowed slightly, sweat had clustered at her hair line, and there was a breathlessness about her I could not place. Her hands clasped tightly in front of her after she bade us goodbyes, her lips lingering too long for my liking on Rose's cheek. I still had not asked about her.

My heart soared when I watched Rose walk through the door, past the statues that stared at the carriage blankly. The clouds were fluffy and grey above us like clusters of smoke and steam hanging around us, a sudden judder and they would dribble rain in warning. The gate creaked in the breeze that pushed and nudged at the chain. A door and a window banged from the top floor and my head snapped up. A few crumbles of rock dribbled down the wall of Erlot Manor.

I scowled as I investigated each window.

The sun was out but the dark hugged the insides of Erlot. Shadows burst at its seams, and it stood still under my gaze. I turned to see Rose looking up at Erlot Manor as well. Her face pale and gaunt in the grey sunlight. Her hair floated in the wind like she was drowning in water. Her lips were red and wet... her eyes shined up at the tallest window. Her mask shivered against her face.

Something was not right.

I made my way inside the carriage after Rose. But when I looked up she was gone.

"Rose?" I called out, looking behind me. I stepped down from the carriage step and walked past a confused Leo.

"Rose?" I looked up at the windows.

I saw a figure in my room.

And then I could see all of them.

At the window so many eyes looked down at me. Old women with their hair hidden men with charred eyes. Children looking lost and pale. Young women with rose petals along their neck.

My heart stopped.

I ran inside.

"What's the matter?" Annabella looked breathless, wide eyes taking me in, taking a step back from me. Matthew followed me inside.

"Rose!" I screamed.

"I'm up here!" Rose called out; her voice somewhat small. I ran up the stairs to Leo's room, and there she was, standing in the middle of the room. "I told you... I can't leave."

I watched her; moments breathed in the space between us.

"I don't understand," I shook my head, "why is this happening?"

Rose didn't say anything. She looked at me. Really looked. Her eyes shining and full. Her face like porcelain, smooth and pale. No concern creased in her brow. Her cheeks dewy and her skin glowing like they did in the moonlight that night. Her hair was still and long and flowing down her back. Her dress grey and hugging her middle perfectly. I drank her in like it was my last fill.

"Try to come down with me, at least," I held my hand out. She took it. Eyes pleading for me.

Don't hope. Not for this.

It will only hurt.

I led her down the stairs again, both of us trying not to think the worst.

As I got to front door, we took a deep breath and soldiered through. Her hand left mine.

"Rose?" I gasped. She was not outside with me. The door had swung shut. The statues staring at me. I bit my lip. I opened the door and stepped inside again. "Rose?"

"I think it's time I showed you something," Annabella appeared at my side, her hand hesitant on my shoulder. I did not say anything. Only followed her down a corridor. Oddly familiar. A door waiting for us at the end.

She opened her mouth to say something. Bu then shut it. And opened the door. I walked down the stone steps, the cold rushing to envelope me in an icy hug. My eyes squinted against the dense black that haunted the basement.

At the bottom of the stairs, I looked over to Annabella, who simply watched my face as she loomed a candle over a box.

I looked at it.

Dense, black, wooden.

A coffin.

I frowned.

My heart stopped.

I leaned forward.

Etched in the wood by hand was:

Rose Mallory Blackwood

"No, this... this can't be-" I looked at her, she only watched me. "No, there's a mistake. This isn't... it can't be! She's upstairs I saw her."

"You've also seen many things since your stay here, haven't you?"

Tears pricked my eyes and my insides felt hollow. Her cold touch, no matter how I tried to warm her. Never leaving the house. Leo.

I gasped; breath escaped me. My feet took me back up the stairs into the marble entrance way, eyes searching frantically for her.

"Rose?!" I all but screamed, my heart aching.

"Dining room!"

I walked inside. What would I find now? But instead, I saw her. As she had always seemed.

I sighed.

"You can't leave."

She nodded and sat at the table. Annabella walked in, looking pale and sombre, holding a tea tray. She poured out two cups of tea. She glanced at Rose, and Rose looked darkly back at her.

"If I can't leave, then I suppose we're stuck here."

I nodded, eyes blurring a little as I realised, I was sat inside the stomach of this infernal house.

"Leo has to stay with his mother," Annabella said. Her eyes not looking at mine.

I nodded again. What was there to say?

I took a teacup from Annabella. Rose bit her lip, eyeing my cup as it rose to my lips. Annabella gave me a guilty look. I took a sip.

I winced at the bitter taste.

"Do you have any sugar?"

THE END

Notes on The Painter's Wife

So many books inspired and affected the way this book was written. Those of note that I feel I should mention (and recommend to you) are:

We Have Always Live in The Castle by Shirley Jackson
The Bloody Chamber by Angela Carter
The Tenant of Wildfell Hall by Anne Bronte
Frankenstein by Mary Shelley
The Picture of Dorian Gray by Oscar Wilde
The Castle of Otranto by Henry Walpole
The Woman in Black by Susan Hill

Zoe McGarrick was born, and grew up, in Bournemouth, England, in 1999. At 10-years-old she decided to finally start reading the Harry Potter books, as she'd been lying to her classmates that she had read them all for years. After finishing the series, she fell in love with literature, reading anything else she could get her hands on. Since then, a dream to be an author began wanting to make someone else feel the way those books did for her.

She graduated with honours from Oxford Brookes University in 2020 with a degree in English Literature. She also has a Masters of Science in Investigative Forensic Psychology. But her biggest achievement was getting a hole in one in crazy golf that time.

She currently lives in Bournemouth, continuing to write more books.

Follow Zoe on
authorzoemcgarrick.com
Instagram & tiktok: @authorzoemcgarrick